THE FARMER AND MRS. LOMBARDI

BOOK 3 IN THE WIVES OF OLD CAPE MAY SERIES

MARYANN DIORIO

maryanndiorio.com

The Farmer and Mrs. Lombardi

by MaryAnn Diorio

THE WIVES OF OLD CAPE MAY Series of Women's Fiction

Book 3: THE FARMER AND MRS. LOMBARDI by MaryAnn Diorio

Published by TopNotch Press, Merchantville, NJ 08109

Softcover Edition: ISBN: 978-1-959699-11-8

Hardcover Edition: ISBN: 978-1-959699-11-9

Electronic Edition: ISBN: 978-1-959699-12-5

AudioBook Edition: ISBN: 978-1-959699-13-2

Library of Congress Control Number: 2024910014

All Scripture quotations are taken from the King James Version of the Bible online at King James Bible Online, www.kingjamesbibleonline.org/.

NOTE: This book is licensed for your personal enjoyment only. This

PRAISE FOR MARYANN DIORIO'S FICTION

The Rabbi and Mrs. Goldstein

"This story gripped my attention from the first page. My heart ached with Miriam Goldstein and her husband Jacob. I rejoiced with them and was encouraged in my own life to trust God for what seems impossible. I highly recommend this book." — *Sharon Beth Brani, Life Coach*

"I haven't read Book 1 yet - I'm not sure why I ordered Book 2 first - but it didn't hinder my understanding at all. This book was a riveting description of how a Jewess converts to Christianity and is shunned by the Jewish community. I learned some interesting details about Jewish settlers in the U.S. The story had me reading well past bed time, and even though there were some uncomfortable emotions portrayed in the book, the author did a great job of bringing things back around to God's care and provision for His children. Very lovely story! -*J. Mac, Reader and Reviewer*

"MaryAnn Diorio's second book in her Cape May series, *The Rabbi and Mrs. Goldstein,* is another captivating story. I love how she intricately develops her characters' personalities, temperaments, and heart-motives. The characters illustrate a gamut of strong emotions including selflessness, selfishness, anger, forgiveness, unconditional love, desperation, and more. The main character, Miriam Goldstein, exhibits a critical aspect of love--compassion--as she attempts to solve sensitive decisions.

The story also explores differing cultural and religious beliefs that offer a challenge to her readers. For instance, when we follow a specific religion, do we do so blindly based on tradition alone, or do we base it on adherence to Biblical truths and standards?

This is an intriguing and stirring story of historical fiction that will hold you captive. If you're like me, you may find it difficult to put down!" — *Christine Strittmatter, Author and Educator*

"This was a delightful story and historically accurate. The characters were realistic and easy to identify with. Being from South Jersey myself, I loved the Cape May,

NJ, setting. I am looking forward to another book in this series." - *Library Lady*

Miracle in Milan

Finalist in the 2022 *Reader's Choice Award for Contemporary Romantic Suspense*.

"Great romance. If you like Christian romance with a touch of suspense this is the book for you. . . A great quick read." — *Swavely Kid, Reader and Reviewer of Fiction*

"Exciting, suspenseful love story.....you won't want to put the book down. *Miracle in Milan* holds your interest from cover to cover. It is a love story that is full of suspense and drama." — *Joan Gangwer, Registered Nutritionist and Avid Reader*

The Madonna of Pisano

"Intense. Gripping. Emotive. Heartrending. And hauntingly beautiful describes *'The Madonna of Pisano'* in a nutshell." — *Diann Flow*

"Excellent characters, dramatic plot. Beautifully written, giving wonderful feeling for the setting in place and time. Emotionally intense situations, satisfying resolution. Among the two or three best novels I have read this year.

Highly recommended." — *Dr. Donn Taylor, Author and Former University Professor*

"Beautiful, touching story of forgiveness and love - - I couldn't read quickly enough, wanting to know what would happen next. Now I am very eager to read the next stories in this series! MaryAnn Diorio has a style of writing that pulls me in - - her descriptions transported me to another time and another country, and I genuinely enjoyed this journey. Highly recommended — FIVE STARS!!" — *Patti Jo Moore*

*"All things work together for good
for those who love the Lord."*

Romans 8: 28

To Jaye and Kathleen Paul

and

To Pam and the late John Schiano . . .

and

*To all parents everywhere who share in the honor and
privilege of raising a child with Down syndrome.
You are heroes in my eyes.*

The Farmer and Mrs. Lombardi

by

MaryAnn Diorio

ednesday, June 20, 1877

LIKE A PROUD MOTHER HEN, Ornella Lombardi gathered her four children around the long oaken table. The tantalizing aroma of Italian spaghetti sauce filled the ample kitchen of the old colonial clapboard house situated on a small farm on the outskirts of Cape May, New Jersey. The farm she and her husband Francesco had purchased shortly after their arrival in America seventeen years before.

Chairs scraped against the worn plank floor as the children took their places at the table. Ranging in age from eight to fourteen, they were the light of Ornella's life. The jewels in her crown. The perfect fulfillment of her lifelong dream to be a mother.

As she leaned over Marco, her youngest, the gold cross necklace, a gift from her maternal grandmother on her eighteenth birthday, dangled from Ornella's neck. *Nonna's* words still rang in her ears: *In times of trouble, always remember the Cross.*

Ornella dismissed the small shiver that skittered across her skin like a bad omen. Times of trouble seemed farther away than her beloved homeland of Italy. She was in America now. The land of promise. Of dreams come true and hopes fulfilled. The land where she could pursue her passion for art without condemnation or criticism.

An anomaly in her native land, she'd never taken well to its centuries-old patriarchal system that allowed men to pursue their professional passions while relegating women to the home and the hearth only to cook, clean, and raise children. Not that she didn't admire and appreciate men. But she, like they, had dreams that extended beyond the homefront. Why should she not be permitted to pursue them simply because she was a woman?

And that is exactly what she planned to do now that her youngest child was in school all day. The prospect of soon being able to paint again and to open the first art gallery in Cape May launched fireworks in her heart.

In leaving her homeland, she'd left societal bias against female artists behind, buried in the soil of her native Abruzzo. Here, in this land of the free, she could control her own life. She could make plans and bring them to fruition. She could pursue her passion.

And nothing would stop her.

Ornella tousled Marco's curly hair and smiled. "Make sure everyone has a napkin, son. The pasta is almost ready."

Eight-year-old Marco returned the smile. "Yes, Mama."

Ornella cleared space on the table for the large spaghetti bowl and then returned to the stove. After dipping a fork into the boiling water to retrieve a strand of spaghetti, she tasted it. Almost done. It would need about another minute of cooking time before it reached the perfect *al dente* texture she preferred.

She smiled in satisfaction. What more could a forty-eight-year-old woman want? Her family was healthy, her marriage was solid, and soon she would make her artistic dream a reality. To her delight, her life was going just as she'd planned.

While waiting for the pasta to finish cooking, Ornella stirred the spaghetti sauce in the big, cast iron pot one last time. She then drained the pasta and placed it in a large, brown ceramic bowl. She poured the rich, thick sauce over it and tossed it to mix. All that remained was a sprinkle of grated Parmesan cheese and the meal would be ready to serve.

"I want to sit next to Mama." Marco pushed aside his ten-year-old sister Caterina as she approached the coveted chair next to Ornella's.

Caterina returned the push. "It's my turn to sit next to Mama. You sat next to her yesterday."

Ornella carried the bowl of spaghetti to the table. "Children! Children! Please stop the bickering. Can we not go one day without any arguing among you?"

Just then her husband Francesco entered the room. "What's going on here?" His face was stern and his voice, booming. At fifty-two years of age, he'd been constrained to cultivate the demeanor of a strict disciplinarian despite his naturally jovial disposition.

"It's my turn to sit next to Mama." Marco whined, his chin jutting forward like a mournful promontory extending beyond the coastline of his mouth.

Caterina folded her arms across her chest. "No, it's not, Papa. It's my turn. Marco sat next to Mama yesterday."

Francesco narrowed his eyes behind the black-rimmed spectacles that rested on his large, Roman nose. "I have an idea. How about you both go to your rooms without dinner, and I will sit next to Mama?" A mischievous smile tickled his lips under a salt-and-pepper mustache.

Ornella chuckled. Her precious Francesco had a

special way of diffusing tension with humor, a trait that had endeared him to her from the very start.

Pouts sinking their faces into the abyss of resignation, Marco and Caterina immediately sat down in their usual seats and remained silent.

Francesco took his place at the head of the table, while Ornella took hers at the opposite end.

"Where's *Nonna*?" Teresa asked about her grandmother, who had come from Italy with her parents.

"She's not feeling well enough to join us at the table." Ornella removed her apron and sat down. "I will take her a plate of pasta after we eat."

"Let's join hands to pray." Francesco led the family in a prayer of thanksgiving and ended it with a resounding *Amen*!

"Amen." The family echoed in unison.

Ornella rose and began filling the plates one by one, starting with Francesco's. As head of an Italian family, honor was due him first as provider and protector. To him went the first serving and the largest portion.

Next, she filled her children's plates. Her heart swelled at the sight of her four beautiful children sitting around the table. Like olive plants, the Bible described them. Teresa, the eldest at fourteen and fair-skinned, resembled her father and had inherited his hazel eyes. Giovanni, the second-born at age twelve, favored Ornella's side of the family, with his dark hair and large, dark brown eyes. Caterina and Marco were a beautiful blend of both parental lines, favoring neither one side nor the other, yet definitely the fruit of both lineages.

Having served everyone, Ornella placed a portion of food on her own plate and sat down again. Her heart warmed as her gaze flew to Francesco. Catching his approving eye, she smiled. God had been good to her. He'd given her the desires of her heart. The man of her dreams. Four children. Two boys. Two girls. The perfect family. All beautiful and healthy.

And soon the Lord would fulfill the desire of her heart to open her own art gallery in Cape May and begin selling her paintings. She released a contented sigh. Life was perfect.

And she would do everything in her power to keep it that way.

"So, there's talk of a railroad strike coming our way." Francesco's voice broke into Ornella's happy thoughts.

Her muscles tensed. "A strike?"

"Yes. In fact, there are rumblings that it has already begun."

"What's a strike, Papa?" Marco spoke through a mouthful of spaghetti.

Papa raised a warning eyebrow. "Don't talk with food in your mouth, Marco. You could choke."

Marco quickly finished chewing and swallowed his pasta. "I'm sorry, Papa."

Francesco acknowledged his apology and continued. "To answer your question, Marco, a strike is an act of protest by employees against the owners of their company. The employees stop working for a while because of an argument over pay or working conditions."

Caterina held her fork in mid-air. "Why are the railroad workers on strike, Papa?"

Francesco shifted his gaze to Caterina. "Their salaries were reduced by ten percent. The workers claim that the company heads are taking too large a share of the profits and leaving the dregs to them. And they're none too happy about it. They are, after all, the ones who do all the hard work."

"I'm going to own the railroad when I grow up," twelve-year-old Giovanni announced, "and I will pay every worker a lot of money."

Francesco nodded his approval. "That's a good goal, my son. Workers should always be treated honestly and with respect. And that includes paying them well."

"I will be the best boss ever, Papa." Giovanni beamed.

Caterina snickered. "I'm sure you will. You've had lots of practice bossing us around."

Giovanni narrowed his eyes. "I don't boss you around."

"Yes, you do." Marco cast an accusatory look toward Giovanni.

"Children." Papa intervened. "It does not please the Lord when we criticize one another."

Ornella leaned forward. "But if there's a strike, how will we get our crops to market?"

Francesco wiped his mouth with his napkin. "That's my main concern. A strike will seriously affect the delivery of our produce to markets between here and Philadelphia. We could use wagons, but the voyage is long, and the crops will likely be destroyed by the heat."

A knot formed in Ornella's stomach. "So what do you think will happen?"

"Well, the strike has already begun and riots have erupted among the workers of the Baltimore & Ohio Railroad in Martinsburg, West Virginia. And unrest is brewing in Baltimore. If a strike indeed takes place there as well, it could spread to the Pennsylvania Railroad and would mean bad news for us farmers here in southern New Jersey."

"But what if the strike doesn't happen, Papa?" Giovanni looked up from his meal, his eyes riveted on his father.

Francesco put down his napkin. "I hope it doesn't, son. But I'm afraid that won't be the case. The workers are quite angry and determined to strike. We farmers can't do much about that. We're dependent on the railroad for our livelihood."

Ornella winced. They were, indeed, dependent on the railroad for their livelihood. Without the railroad, they would not be able to get their produce to Philadelphia and the many small towns along the way.

Their income would drop drastically. Perhaps she should open her gallery sooner rather than later.

"You're the best farmer in the whole world, Papa." Marco made a valiant attempt to return to his father's good graces. "I want to be just like you when I grow up."

Francesco laughed. "Thank you, Marco. But you are my son, and you are prejudiced."

"I'm not prejudiced, Papa." Marco spoke with firm conviction and then wrinkled his nose. "What does *prejudiced* mean, Papa?"

"It means leaning toward one opinion over another."

"Then I'm leaning toward you, Papa." He gave a sheepish smile. "And I'm telling the truth."

"As well you should. You should always stand for truth regardless of where it comes from."

The conversation about the strike had stolen Ornella's appetite. What would they do if the money stopped coming in? How would they pay the hired hands? And how long would the strike last?

Teresa interrupted Ornella's rambling thoughts. "Mama, may I have more pasta?" Teresa held up her dish, a sweet smile on her face.

Hoping she'd be able to feed her children as long as the strike lasted, Ornella gave her daughter another generous serving of spaghetti. "After dinner, Teresa, I would like you and Caterina to wash the dishes and clean up the kitchen while I take Nonna her dinner. "

"Why do we girls always have to clean up the

kitchen?" Caterina whined. "Why can't Marco and Giovanni help us once in a while?"

Fourteen-year-old Teresa vehemently supported her younger sister's argument. "Yes, Mama. Why do we girls always have to do the cleaning?"

Ornella hesitated. Her daughters were right. Why did housework always fall to the women in the family? Had she unintentionally set the precedent? Was she unwittingly passing on the traditions of her ancestors without thinking them through? "I agree with you, Teresa. From now on, I will require that Marco and Giovanni take a turn at cleaning the kitchen."

Giovanni grunted. "Then you have to make Teresa and Caterina take a turn at taking out the trash."

Teresa pre-empted her mother's response. "It's a deal." She gave her brothers a triumphant smirk that was followed only by their loud protests.

"Now go on, children," Ornella prodded. "I need to check in on Nonna and bring her some pasta."

WEDNESDAY, June 20, 1877

As ORNELLA RETRIEVED a dish for her aging mother from the cupboard, a mewing sound came from outside the back door. Still holding Mama's dish in her hand, she opened the back door. A beautiful black and white stray kitten stood on the doorstep, looking up at her with pleading eyes.

Ornella's heart stirred. She quickly placed her mother's dish on the counter and stooped toward the kitten to pet her. "You poor thing. You must be hungry." Against her better judgment, Ornella picked up the kitten and brought the tiny creature inside. "Come. I'll get you some milk."

With her free hand, she poured some milk into a small bowl and placed it on the floor. Then she gently lowered the kitten to the floor, next to the bowl of milk. The poor, starving creature lapped up the milk like a ravenous tiger, licking every inch of the bowl and leaving not a single drop.

Despite her scrawniness, she was a lovely kitten. The sharp contrast of white against black fur offered stunning artistic possibilities. Perhaps when the little creature had had his fill, Ornella would do some sketches for a later painting. She could sell it as wall art for a child's room. She smiled to herself. Unless Marco claimed it first.

"My, my, little one, you were starving, weren't you?" Ornella gave her a second bowl of milk, which the kitten devoured as quickly as he had the first.

Just then Marco came up beside Ornella. "Mama, where did the kitten come from?"

"The poor creature was on the back doorstep. I heard mewing, opened the door, and found him there."

"Can we keep him?"

"First we must find out if he belongs to one of the neighbors." She turned toward Marco. "But I can't do that now. I have to bring Nonna her dinner. So would you mind taking care of the kitten while I do that?"

Marco broke into a broad grin. "I don't mind at all, Mama."

As Marco occupied himself with the kitten, Ornella washed her hands. She then prepared a plate of spaghetti for her mother and brought it to her.

Ornella found the elderly woman sitting in a rocking chair in the spare bedroom that had become her personal oasis. A hand-crocheted, navy blue blanket covered her lap, and a large patchwork pillow supported her back. At seventy-six years of age, Mama had grown frail. Wrinkles lined her round face, and her white hair had grown thin. Blue veins accentuated the backs of her hands. But despite her weakened condition, she was still sharp of mind—and also of tongue. She grunted when Ornella entered the room.

"Mama, I've brought you some dinner." Ornella offered her her cheeriest voice.

Her mother drew her eyebrows together. "What did you cook?"

Ornella smiled. "Your favorite. Spaghetti with salsa." She placed the dish on a small table next to Mama's rocking chair, together with a fork, spoon, and napkin.

Mama crossed her arms. "I'm not hungry."

Ornella sat down on the bed. "Since when are you not hungry? Do you not feel well?"

The old woman rocked faster. "I feel fine."

"Then why aren't you hungry?" Sometimes it took every ounce of Ornella's patience to humor her mother.

Mama glared at her. "Can't an old woman not be hungry when she chooses?"

Ornella released a sigh. There had never been any use in arguing with Mama. Ever since Ornella was a young girl, she'd tried and failed. The woman was as stubborn as the orneriest mule. And now that she was elderly, she'd become even more stubborn. "I suppose at your age, Mama, a woman can do whatever she wants."

The words seemed to pacify her mother. She relented and chuckled. "Maybe I will try a bit of your spaghetti." A twinkle appeared in Mama's eye. "I can't deny it smells really good." Mama took the plate from the table. "And you are a wonderful cook."

"I have you to thank, Mama. You taught me everything I know."

"Well, not everything. Your father taught you a few things."

A pang of remorse flitted through Ornella. Any mention of her alcoholic father stirred up painful memories. He'd put Mama through a lot. Having been abandoned by him when Ornella was only six years old, Mama had raised her alone while working as a seamstress in the little Italian fishing village of Vasto on the Adriatic Sea. Yet, Mama had never stopped loving him.

"Do you wish your life had been different, Mama?"

Mama's eyes misted. "Every single day. Especially for your sake. I regret that you grew up without a father." Her gaze grew wistful as it found a place beyond Ornella.

Ornella swallowed hard. Growing up without a father had caused her great suffering. But she said nothing. She did not want to hurt Mama any more than she'd already been hurt.

The old woman returned her gaze to her daughter. "But life goes on, my dear daughter. Looking back only makes a bad situation worse."

Ornella swallowed the lump in her throat. How did Mama do it? How did she survive with such sorrow in her heart? If Francesco abandoned her, Ornella would fall apart.

"Mama, after I return from my knitting circle meeting tomorrow, I plan to take the children to the beach. Would you like to come with us and sit in the sun for a while?"

Mama nodded. "I would like that very much." And with that, the old woman's crankiness disappeared as she plunged into her dinner with relish.

CHAPTER

TWO

Thursday, June 21, 1877

THE NEXT MORNING, Ornella walked the half mile from the farm to Christian Community Church in Cape May for her weekly knitting circle and Bible study meeting. She loved spending a few hours each week in fellowship with the special ladies of the group, all sisters in Christ and members of her church. Loretta Vye, Miriam Goldstein, Ebony Phillips, Cholena Cohanzick, and Clarissa Steubens—all had been there for her over the years, giving her wise counsel. As the youngest member of the group and the least spiritually mature,

Ornella looked up to them as mentors. They added such richness to her life through their wisdom, unique personalities, and special talents. She smiled just thinking of them.

Holding her pale blue parasol over her head to shade herself from the hot sun, Ornella breathed in the warm morning air. With the family farm situated just on the outskirts of town, her walk to the church was normally a pleasant one. On a good day, she could cover the distance at a leisurely pace in about thirty minutes.

But today's early morning heat slowed her down a bit. Or was it that she'd awakened with an upset stomach? Had she eaten something that did not agree with her?

She dismissed the thought, glad that she was feeling better now. No matter the weather, she needed this weekly break that provided both a physical and a spiritual respite from the demands of raising four active children. Raising children in one's forties was far different from raising them in one's twenties. Besides, cultural assertions to the contrary, she needed more than motherhood in her life.

Other women of her generation were awakening to that fact, too, realizing that they were persons in their own right, with dreams and desires of their own outside the home. Why did societal norms insist that a woman be satisfied with running a home, raising children, and nothing more? Although generations of women before her had been satisfied with that arrangement, she could never be. One day her children would be grown. Then what?

She sighed. Old-fashioned cultural traditions lingered long and died hard.

No, she needed more in life than raising children and making a home, as wonderful and important as those occupations were. God had given her great artistic talent. She would not bury it, as so many women before her had done. Living in America should make it easier for her to follow and fulfill her dream. The country's ideological support of independence would help her carve a smoother path for herself.

Indeed, had not Elizabeth Blackwell accomplished the great feat of becoming the first female doctor to graduate with a degree in medicine only twenty-eight years before, and with the academic rank of first in her class? Ornella drew in a deep breath. Yes, like Elizabeth Blackwell, she would allow nothing to stop her or to stand in her way of achieving her dream. Her life was hers to control, and she would not relinquish that control to anyone.

The smell of salt tickled her nose as she drew closer to the shore. She breathed in the salubrious salt air that cleared both her lungs and her mind. No wonder so many people came to the sea to cure their ailments, both physical and mental.

As Ornella approached Cape May town center,

she came alive at the prospect of being with her sisters in Christ once again. And she especially didn't want to miss today's study. Clarissa would be teaching on trusting God. Ornella could never get enough of that teaching. Ever since her father abandoned her, trust had always been difficult for her.

Despite her many years of following Christ, Ornella still found it difficult to surrender the reins of her life completely to God. Yet, she wanted to do the right thing. But letting go of control filled her with apprehension and dread. What if God failed her?

Just as her earthly father had failed her.

She stifled the painful memory.

In the distance, a horse-drawn wagon approached from the opposite direction. As it drew closer, William, one of the farmhands on the family farm, waved at her. William was the first farmhand Francesco had hired. He'd been a faithful employee for over fifteen years.

He slowed down as he drew closer. "Why, good mornin', Miz Lombardi. How you be doin' on this fine but hot mornin'?"

Ornella chuckled. "I'm doing just like the morning, William. Fine, but hot."

"And where be you headed, ma'am?"

"To my weekly Bible study."

William's face broke into a broad grin, his perfectly straight white teeth shining bright against his rich, chocolate skin. "Praise the Lawd! T'ain't nothin' like studyin' God's Word."

"You're right, William."

"Would you like me to drive you there?"

"Thank you, William, but I don't have far to go. Besides, you're traveling in the opposite direction."

"I gladly be willin' to turn around, ma'am." His eyes reflected his kind heart.

"I know you would, William. You're a kind man. But thank you, nonetheless. You go on ahead. I'm sure Francesco could use your expert help in the fields."

He gazed ahead. "I suppose so. What with this strike gettin' worse, some of the men be leavin' to find work in other states. Mr. Lombardi be worryin' about us bein' short of men to work the fields."

Ornella's stomach clenched. "Francesco mentioned something about a strike last night. Has it gotten worse?"

William frowned. "Plenty worse, ma'am. There be fightin' in the streets of Philadelphia last night."

Ornella's heart clenched. "Oh, my! It's gotten that bad, has it?"

"Yes, ma'am. Pretty bad. There be two men killed already."

Ornella pressed her hand against her throat. "Dear me, William! I didn't realize it was that serious. What can be done?"

"Prayin' be the best thing, ma'am." William's face bore the lines of worry around his eyes. "Only the Lawd can fix this." He sighed. "Well, I best be goin'. Mr. Lombardi be expectin' me anytime now."

"Thank you for your kindness, William. Have a good day."

"You as well, ma'am." He nodded, smiled, and then, administering a light tap of the whip to the ground next to the horse, proceeded toward the farm.

THURSDAY, June 21, 1877

As ICY FINGERS of fear crept up her spine, Ornella took in a deep breath and resumed her walk. No wonder Francesco had seemed especially troubled this morning after reading the newspaper. He hadn't told her about the killings. Surely so as not to worry her. But, knowing her husband as well as she did, he was certainly worried. This kind of situation could easily escalate and spread outside the city of Philadelphia and into the rural areas. Her breath caught. She would ask the women of her knitting circle to pray.

In a few moments, she reached the edge of town. From there, it was only two blocks to the church. Several horse-drawn buggies crowded the street, their wheels grinding against the gravel as the horses clip-clopped along, whipping up dust that burned her nostrils.

Ornella shifted her parasol from her right shoulder to her left and wiped the beads of perspiration from her brow. Rounding the corner of the old country road leading to downtown, she made her way onto Lafayette Street. Already summer tourists had begun to crowd the sidewalks. Most were headed to the beach, while others set out to explore the many shops lining the sidewalks. She nodded and smiled at several of them as they passed by.

Despite the disruption they caused to the locals' quiet life, the tourists provided much needed income for the quaint seaside town. Income that sustained them throughout the cold, barren months of winter. Income that helped the family farm remain solvent. During the summer months, local restaurants purchased large volumes of tomatoes, cucumbers, and blueberries from the farm to feed the huge influx of vacationers. Ornella and Francesco counted on that income to make ends meet during the winter months.

But the railroad strike had kept many tourists away, badly hurting the economy of the area. Ornella bit her lip. Most of them traveled to Cape May by rail. If the trains stopped running, the tourist population would dwindle.

And so would the family's income.

Despite the intense heat, a shudder ran through her. Better to think good thoughts, as the Good Book commanded.

Ornella's mind drifted to Mama. Ornella had checked on her before she left. The dear woman was in better spirits this morning, having eaten a hearty meal the night before and having gotten a good night of rest. She'd even offered to feed the children their breakfast. Ornella whispered a prayer of thanks. Over the years, Mama had been a huge help to her in raising the children.

From Mama her mind shifted to the stray kitten. Marco had taken the creature under his wings and, after determining that the cat did not belong to any of the neighbors and that she was a female, had given her the name Sofia—explaining that the name meant wisdom—and claiming that the kitten had been very wise in choosing to stop at their home for a meal. Ornella smiled. Marco had begged her to keep the kitten as a pet and, unable to resist his charming ways, she'd quickly conceded.

She chuckled at the memory. Marco was the most persuasive one of her brood of children. He could convince a king to exchange his royal palace for a humble tent without blinking an eye. She would include her son in her painting of the kitten.

As she approached the church, she stopped to allow a carriage to pass before crossing the street, comforting herself with the thought that now that Marco was becoming more self-sufficient, she could proceed with her dream to focus on her art and to open her art gallery.

Straight ahead stood the little storefront she'd had

her eye on for a while now as the perfect location for her gallery. A *For Rent* sign sat prominently in the window. Her heart leapt. She would stop by on the way home after Bible study to inquire about the monthly rental fee.

With the railroad strike growing worse, she needed to do something to contribute to the family income. Already Francesco talked of drawing on their meager life savings to support their family. She could always take in some sewing or work in one of the local shops. But art was her passion. She'd rather paint for a living than do anything else.

But selling art did not provide consistent income, at least not at first. It would take some time to develop a clientèle. Would she have to toss her plans to develop an art career out the window?

No. Never. Not if she could help it.

A group of chattering tourists strolled in her direction on the sidewalk, oblivious to her approach. Ornella sidestepped them just in time to avoid a collision. Releasing a sigh of frustration, she crossed Lafayette Street at the crosswalk and waved to the postman as he walked by, carrying his leather satchel filled with the day's mail.

When she reached the other side of the street, a sudden, unexpected wave of nausea overwhelmed her. She clutched her quilted bag of knitting supplies and stopped to lean against a nearby tree, trying to get her bearings. What was going on? This was the second time this morning she'd experienced nausea. Could it be the spaghetti sauce she'd cooked last night? But no one else in the family had complained of feeling sick.

The nausea soon passed, leaving her stomach quivering on the inside. Taking in a deep breath, she continued toward the church. Upon arrival, she would have a cup of peppermint tea. Clarissa, a retired pastor's wife and the leader of the knitting circle, always had tea and coffee ready, together with some homemade muffins, for the six ladies who attended each week. But today, Ornella would skip the muffins.

As she reached the church, blossoming petunias bobbed in the light breeze, their bright colors shimmering in the morning sunlight. In a nearby oak tree, a robin chirped at the top of its lungs. But the usually sweet scent of honeysuckle gracing the front of the white stucco church now made her stomach roil.

She paused in front of the peaceful, old eighteenth-century building. White streaks lined its green, splintered shutters, buffeted from the severe storms and hurricanes that had rampaged the area during the past century. Ornella loved the little church. It was the place where, at Loretta Vye's invitation, she'd first learned of her need to be born again and where she'd accepted Christ as her Savior and Lord.

And she'd remained there ever since.

As Ornella reached the foot of the front steps,

Loretta and Miriam hurried toward her from the opposite direction.

Loretta laughed. "I see you're late, too, Ornella. I thought we were the only tardy ones." Loretta cast a mischievous glance at Miriam. "We have a good excuse, don't we Miriam?" She chuckled. "After all, two old women at the half-century mark deserve a little mercy, don't you think?"

Ornella laughed. "And so does an old woman approaching the half-century mark who is still raising four active children."

Miriam placed a hand on Ornella's forearm and smiled. "I agree wholeheartedly. Raising little ones can sap all of one's strength. Take it from one who raised three rambunctious children."

Ornella smiled at the truth of Miriam's words.

"Well, let's hurry. We don't want to keep Clarissa waiting." Loretta hooked her arm into Miriam's. "Age before beauty," she quipped to Ornella.

Ornella laughed and followed the two ladies up the steps and into the church. But as she entered the front door, her world began to spin as another wave of nausea struck her even more forcefully this time. She clung to the doorknob, resting her head against the door while taking deep breaths.

Loretta rushed to Ornella's side. "Ornella, are you all right? You look pale."

"I'm fine. Really. My stomach's a bit upset. Must be something I ate." Ornella raised her head. "You two go on ahead. I'll be in shortly." Ornella motioned to Loretta and Miriam to proceed without her. "I'll just sit in the sanctuary for a few moments to rest and join you shortly."

Miriam knit her brows. "I don't think we should leave you here alone."

"Really, I'm fine. Don't worry. I'll join you in a few moments."

A worrisome frown wrinkled Miriam's forehead. "If you haven't joined us within ten minutes, I'll be back to check on you."

"Fair enough." Ornella forced a tentative smile.

While Loretta and Miriam made their way to the knitting circle room, Ornella quickly found a pew and sat down. Her heart raced and her pulse quickened. Droplets of perspiration lined her forehead, and shivers ran through her body. She reviewed her food intake from the previous day. Nothing unusual. Nothing that was spoiled. Besides, no one else in the family had gotten sick, and they'd all eaten the same food.

As she pondered her activities of the past few days, it struck her that she hadn't had her flow yet this month. But at her age, and fast approaching menopause, being a few days late was nothing of major concern.

Yet, a disturbing thought niggled at the back of her mind. A thought she did not want to entertain. A thought that made every part of her body and soul cringe.

She drew in a long, deep breath as yet another wave of nausea overwhelmed her. She rested her forehead on the back of the pew in front of her and closed her eyes.

If she didn't know any better, she'd think that she was pregnant.

CHAPTER

THREE

Thursday, June 21, 1877

AFTER A FEW MOMENTS, Ornella collected herself, rose from the pew, and headed toward the knitting circle room at the back of the church. The waves of nausea had subsided, leaving behind only a slight quiver in her belly and a clamminess in her hands.

Brushing aside all nervous thoughts of pregnancy, she took her place at the round table.

"You look much better." Miriam leaned toward Ornella and smiled. "You had me worried there for a minute."

Ornella nodded. "I don't know what came over me. I

felt fine until I got closer to the church. Then I had to stop and lean against a tree. I thought I would pass out."

Loretta cast a sweet smile her way. "You couldn't be pregnant, could you?"

Ornella's heart lurched. The mere thought of that possibility terrified her. "I can't be."

Having overheard the snippet of conversation between Ornella and Loretta, Ebony Phillips grinned and shook a warning index finger at Ornella. "My great-aunt Tilly had a bonus baby when she was forty-six years old. And that, after her other children were already married with families of their own." Ebony laughed. "Talk about a surprise."

Ornella could do without that kind of surprise. "I can't be pregnant. I've already begun the change." Although Ornella loved these women, their well-meaning comments unnerved her.

Ebony shook her head. "Great-Aunt Tilly thought she'd gone through the change, too. How wrong she was!"

Clarissa stood to her feet and glanced sympathetically toward Ornella. "Well, ladies, I know that talk about babies can be pleasant, but we do need to start our meeting. Let's open with prayer."

As Clarissa prayed, Ornella's mind wrestled with fear. If she were, indeed, pregnant, how would she manage at her age? And how would she and Francesco provide for another child? Even now Francesco was worried that the railroad strike could threaten their livelihood. What would he do if they were expecting another baby? The farm barely brought in enough revenue to feed a family of four children without adding another mouth to feed. She swallowed the hard lump in her throat. And what about her dream of returning to painting and opening an art gallery?

Clarissa's voice broke through Ornella's scrambled thoughts. "Today's lesson, ladies, is on trusting God. We will begin by reading from Proverbs 3: 5 and 6: *'Trust in the LORD with all thine heart; and lean not unto thine own understanding. In all thy ways acknowledge him, and he shall direct thy paths.'* Let's discuss what it means to trust in the Lord."

Although the topic was just what Ornella needed, her mind kept wandering like a stubborn sheep bent on escaping the pasture. Why did she find it so hard to lasso her thoughts to Christ, as Scripture commanded her to do? Was her imagination more vivid than that of most? She couldn't deny she had an inborn tendency to worry. Not unusual among Italians. Maybe it was their Mediterranean temperament, or maybe a generational curse. Whatever it was, it was not a good thing.

Clarissa continued. "Would anyone like to share a testimony of your experience trusting God in a hopeless situation? Did you find it difficult to do? What challenges did you face?"

Loretta was the first to speak. "When my Edward

died suddenly, I was in a state of shock, especially when I discovered that he had left me penniless. I became terribly anxious and could not sleep at night, imagining the worst. Being childless and alone, I had nowhere to turn." Her eyes brimmed with tears. "But the Lord provided everything I needed. He taught me to trust Him during that difficult time. And He proved faithful. He made a way where there seemed to be no way. He made possible what seemed impossible. I will be forever grateful to Him."

Clarissa nodded. "Yes, Loretta, how well I remember that very difficult time in your life. God showed Himself mighty on your behalf as we prayed and prayed."

"Amen." Loretta lifted her hands and looked heavenward in a gesture of thanksgiving and praise. Tears of gratitude trickled down her face amid exclamations of hallelujah from the group of ladies.

Miriam Goldstein spoke next. "When I faced the truth that Yeshua is the Messiah and I accepted Him as my Savior, my husband Jacob divorced me and my family disowned me. It was the darkest period of my life. For months, I did not see my husband nor my children and grandchildren. I felt utterly abandoned and alone.

"But I knew that Yeshua was with me. He did the miraculous for me. He turned what Satan meant for evil into great good. My rabbi husband eventually recognized that Yeshua is, indeed, the Jews' long-awaited Messiah. Jacob and I were reunited, and now we serve the Lord together in this very church. Only God could have done that. He is faithful to His Word and perfectly trustworthy. Praise His Holy Name!"

One by one, each of the ladies shared a testimony of God's faithfulness in times of great trial. And with each one, Ornella's heart was stirred.

But when her turn came to share a testimony about trusting God, she was at a loss. Throughout her life, she'd made her own decisions. Her own plans. And they had all turned out just as she'd planned. So where was the need to trust God? He'd given her a mind, hadn't He? And wasn't that mind to be used to plan her own life as she thought best? Did trusting God with her life mean making no decisions for herself?

She swallowed hard, trying to formulate a cohesive response, but coherent thoughts eluded her. After all, she hadn't consulted God when making decisions, especially major ones. She'd trusted her own desires, dreams, and passions. And everything had turned out well.

She searched her past. "Well, I suppose I trusted in God when He led me to America, although I had no relationship with the Lord at the time. Yes, I believed in Jesus and knew that He was the Son of God who died for my sins. But I simply gave mental assent—not heart assent—to that truth. And I did so because my mother and grandmother before me had done so. So, when I left Italy, I left as an unbeliever, but thinking I was a believer." She lowered her eyes and then raised them again. "A very dangerous place to be. I was not aware of my true spiritual state.

"It was a scary decision for me to leave Italy and all I'd known all my life to come to a land whose language I could not speak and whose customs I did not understand. As I look back, I can see that God took care of me even then. Despite my unregenerate condition, He had mercy on me and protected me." Ornella swallowed hard as the depth of the Lord's love for her overwhelmed her.

"And He always will take care of you." Clarissa's steadied gaze locked onto Ornella's like a premonition of sorts.

A shiver coursed through Ornella's veins. Did Clarissa know something she did not?

Clarissa turned to the group. "And now on to our prayer and worship time. Are there any prayer requests?"

"Yes." Ornella spoke first. "You may have heard of the railroad strike that has broken out in Philadelphia. It has spread from its starting point with the Baltimore-Ohio Railroad in West Virginia and has now affected the Pennsylvania Railroad as well. It has already begun to affect our farm and our livelihood. Please pray that it will end soon. We use the railroad to ship our produce to Philadelphia and to towns along the way. If the railways stop running, our income will come to an abrupt stop, too."

Cholena leaned forward. "My brother-in-law works

on the railroad and told me of the strike. He said that tension is increasing not only among the strikers but also among those whose businesses rely on railroad transportation. And that includes several of the businesses here in Cape May."

"That's right." Ebony chimed in. "My son's hardware store experienced a shortage of nails and other items that are shipped in by rail from Maryland and other points west."

Clarissa concurred. "And the sewing supplies store in town hasn't received a shipment of fabric in over a week."

Other instances of the negative effects of the strike travelled from one lady to the next until Clarissa eventually united everyone in prayer. "Lord Jesus, we place this strike and everyone involved in it in Your capable hands. We ask that You would put an end to it before anyone else gets hurt. We speak Your peace into the situation, Lord. Make a way for a resolution where there seems to be no way. We trust in You, O God, to hear and answer this prayer that we make in the mighty Name of Jesus. Amen."

All the ladies responded with a resounding "Amen!"

For the next thirty minutes, the group worshipped the Lord with hymns and prayed for one another's needs. Afterward, they stopped for refreshments before working on their knitting projects.

By the time the morning session was over, Ornella's

queasiness had left and she was back to normal. Physically, at least.

But doubt still gnawed at her mind, forcing her to meditate more than ever on the Bible lesson of the morning. Trust in the Lord. Lean not to her own understanding. Acknowledge Him in all her ways, and He would direct her steps.

But the hard part was not knowing where those steps would lead.

~

THURSDAY AFTERNOON, June 21, 1877

ON THE WAY home from Bible study, Ornella stopped at the little storefront with the rental sign in the window. Although financially this was not the best time for her to rent a place for her art gallery, it wouldn't hurt to inquire. Doing so would give her an idea as to future costs and how best to prepare.

A little bell tinkled as she walked through the door.

"Good afternoon." An elderly man with a white mustache extended a hand in greeting. "I'm Whitney Burroughs. What may I do for you this fine day?"

"Good afternoon. My name is Ornella Lombardi. I am a local artist looking to open a small art gallery here in town sometime in the future, and your *For Rent* sign in the window caught my eye."

"What a boon that will be to Cape May! Each year, more and more people are learning about our little jewel of a town and making it their vacation spot. I think this is the perfect location for an art gallery."

"I agree. It's a dream I've held for a long time. But, frankly, at the moment, I am simply in the exploration stage."

"Are you from Cape May?"

"Yes. My husband and I came from Italy and have lived here for several years. We own a little farm on the outskirts of town, about a half mile from here."

"I hear that Italy is a very beautiful place."

"It is." Ornella smiled. "You should visit one day."

"I would love to." The man sighed. "And now to your matter. This building was built by my father when I was just a child. My father housed his hardware store here for decades before he died. I spent many happy hours as a young boy working with him here."

"How special!"

"It was, indeed. I eventually took over the business. But now that I'm getting up in years, it's time for me to settle down a bit." He laughed. "At least, that's what my wife tells me." He grew wistful. "My wife and I have no children of our own to take over the business, so we've decided to rent out the space."

"I see. I'm interested in learning more."

"Well, feel free to take a look around." He waved a hand in the direction of the open space behind her.

Ornella turned and walked through the large empty room. There was plenty of space on the walls to hang her paintings. Plus, adequate floor space would make it possible to display easels to hold paintings during art shows. She also had enough room to feature other local artists as the opportunity arose.

Encouraged by the appearance of the space and by Mr. Burroughs' enthusiasm, Ornella thanked him. "What are you charging for rent?"

"Sixty-five dollars per month. The unit includes an indoor commode and a small kitchen at the back."

"That sounds very reasonable." The place was exactly what Ornella was looking for. Now all she needed was to obtain Francesco's approval and to find a way to rent it.

"Thank you so very much, Mr. Burroughs. I will discuss this with my husband and get back to you. When will the unit be available?"

"As soon as you need it. Just give me a day's notice, and I'll have it ready for you."

"Wonderful. I wish I could give you a definite answer now, but I must first discuss the matter with my husband. I will get back to you by the end of the week."

"Excellent." He extended a hand toward her. "It was a pleasure to meet you, Mrs. Lombardi. I look forward to hearing from you later in the week." He chuckled. "But don't wait too long. This is prime rental space, and someone else may beat you to it."

Ornella's stomach tightened as she shook his hand. "I'll keep that in mind, Mr. Burroughs."

She smiled and left, hoping against hope that the lovely space would fall to her.

CHAPTER
FOUR

*T*hursday, *June 21, 1877*

ON HER WAY HOME, Ornella excitedly considered the many possibilities the rental space would offer her. It was located in the center of the downtown district, the area that attracted most of the tourists, not to mention the area frequented by most of the locals during the winter months. Nestled between two popular businesses—a gift shoppe and a yarn shoppe—it would draw customers who frequented those places as well.

Already she imagined how she would arrange the paintings she'd completed before her children were born. Paintings of animals and flowers. Still lifes of fresh produce from the farm and lovely seascapes of the surrounding ocean and bay. Subjects to appeal to a variety of art lovers. She would even include some of the paintings she'd done in Italy and brought with her. Paintings of the breath-taking Adriatic Sea and the colorful Italian villages dotting the coastline.

Now that all of her children were growing up and in school, she would have time to fill more canvases with her passion for art. She would add additional paintings, including the one of Marco and his kitten Sofia. She would also supplement the family income by inviting other local artists to display and sell their art on a commission basis. Her heart soared at the many ideas whirling around in her head.

She imagined her first customers entering the gallery and marveling at the lovely paintings. They would move from piece to piece, exploring every facet of each painting and commenting on it. Finally, they would buy her entire inventory.

Ornella laughed at her wild imaginings. But wasn't the imagination the seat of hope? Things were falling into place, just as she'd planned. Her dream was finally coming true.

She turned onto the road that led to the farm. But what if someone else rented the space first? Mr. Burroughs would certainly not wait around for her. Nor should he.

The thought of losing that precious space disturbed

her. She would discuss the matter with Francesco later that night after dinner.

THURSDAY, June 21, 1877

THE REST of Ornella's day passed with no further episodes of nausea. She took Mama and the children to the beach, and they enjoyed a wonderful time. She and Mama basked in the afternoon sunshine while the children frolicked in the sparkling ocean water. By dinnertime, Ornella gave no more thought to the nausea incident, so absorbed was she in preparing dinner and getting the younger children ready for bed.

Once the children and Mama were asleep, Ornella settled into the rocking chair in her bedroom. Francesco sat in a chair beside her, his face buried in the evening newspaper.

"Francesco?"

"Yes?" He raised his head.

"On the way home from Bible study, I stopped by a little store downtown that had a *For Rent* sign in the window."

"And?"

"It would make the perfect place for my art gallery." Her heart racing, she tried to read his face.

"What is the monthly rent?"

""It's only sixty-five dollars a month. And it includes an indoor commode and a small kitchen in the back."

He thought for a moment. "The rent is not bad, but how can we pay for it?"

"I had hoped we could take it from our life savings until I sold enough paintings to pay the rent from sales alone."

His face grew pensive. "I don't think now is the right time, Ornella. The railroad strike is seriously affecting the sale of our crops. We've already had to dip into our life savings just to make ends meet. I'm afraid to take any more money unnecessarily."

Ornella bristled. "Unnecessarily? Don't you realize that my art is a necessity to me?"

Francesco's jaw twitched. "I'm not saying your art is not important, Ornella, but feeding our children takes a higher priority."

"But perhaps, for that very reason, this *is* the right time. What if I sold enough paintings to offset the losses from the railroad strike and to give us extra income?"

"That would take a lot of sales in a very short amount of time. Besides, people aren't buying art these days. They are still recovering from the financial panic of 1873."

"But the art market is flourishing in New York City."

"But we're not in New York City, Ornella."

Impatience edged his voice. "We're in Cape May. Who comes here other than vacationers?"

"Francesco, don't you see? Vacationers sometimes have connections. Who knows but that someone from New York City might come here and discover my art?"

A repentant smile crossed his face. "You've always been the eternal optimist." He grew thoughtful. "Were it not for the strike, I would say yes. But I'm quite concerned about what this strike has done to our income. I don't know what the future holds, but I want to be prepared. Selling art is not like selling food. People can't survive on art alone. They need food for their bellies."

And food for their souls. "So, is your answer no?"

"I hate to say no to you, Ornella. But I'm afraid it's the wisest course of action for the time being."

Her heart sank.

"Perhaps another space will become available when the time is right."

"I hope so." But she doubted it. Mr. Burroughs' space was exactly what she was looking for.

"Let's pray and see what the Lord will do. Only He knows the future."

The future. Like Ebony's words earlier that day, Francesco's sounded like a bad omen. What did the future hold? As far as she was concerned, the future held what she planned it to hold. The fulfillment of her artistic dream.

While Francesco returned to his newspaper, Ornella's

thoughts drifted once again toward her nausea episodes. She still had not shared them with Francesco. There was no need to. Like most of her worries, this would amount to nothing as well.

But that night, as she lay at her husband's side, the fearful thought once again nibbled at her mind, tormenting her and robbing her of all peace. Could she indeed be pregnant?

Ebony's warning, while couched in humor, still haunted her. What if Ebony's words proved true? What if Ornella's experience would be a repeat of Ebony's middle-aged aunt? What if she were really carrying a "bonus baby," as Ebony had called the unexpected child? What would Ornella do then?

What-ifs bombarded Ornella's mind like so many fiery darts piercing her soul and robbing her of peace. Every attempt to dodge them resulted only in placing herself directly in the line of fire of new ones. Would she be forced to give up her dream? To abandon all hope of ever opening an art gallery and selling her art? Would she ever experience the professional freedom and satisfaction she longed for?

She shut her eyes tight to hide from her fear. No. She couldn't possibly be pregnant. Having a child at her age would complicate her perfect life. Her well-ordered life. The life that, so far, had gone according to her perfect plan. A plan she would continue to enforce, no matter what the cost. She would remain in control of her life. If she didn't, her world would fall apart, just as it had when Papa left. She would not let that happen again. For her very survival, she had to remain in control.

Ornella stared at the ceiling, Francesco's incessant snoring aggravating her nerves in a way it usually did not. The clock had already struck midnight, and still she had not slept. She'd come so close to telling him about the episodes of nausea she'd experienced that morning, but then she'd decided against it. Why trouble him with something that was of no consequence when he had so many other things on his mind? Like the strike and the trouble it portended for the farm and the family. A little upset stomach was no big thing compared to that.

She turned onto her side and gazed out the tall bedroom window. A full moon shone in the indigo sky, casting swaths of milky white light through the sheer lace curtains. She should have her monthly any time now. Her chest tightened. While she'd been late before, she'd never been this late. She drew in a deep breath. Perhaps she should visit Ramona the midwife. Ramona would reassure her that all was well and that she could go on with her life.

Yes. Tomorrow she would visit Ramona to free herself from these silly worries and to set her mind at ease.

But as Ornella rolled onto her back again, she had an uneasy feeling that instead of reassurance, Ramona would only confirm her fears.

CHAPTER
FIVE

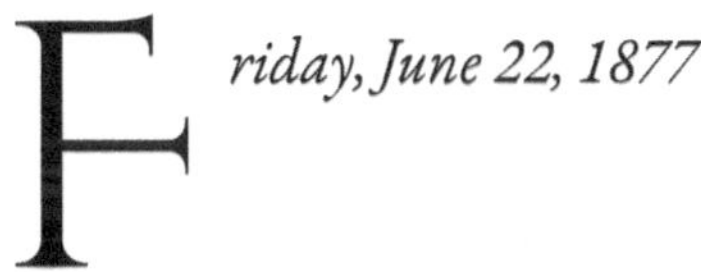

Friday, June 22, 1877

"I HAVE good news for you, Ornella." Ramona the midwife smiled, her eyes wide with joy. "You are with child."

Like a cannonball exploding from a cannon, the words struck Ornella's heart, knocking the wind out of her. She gasped. "I can't be!" Surely it was all a dream. A bad dream. "I can't be." She repeated the words as the fog of incredulity darkened her mind.

Ramona placed a hand on Ornella's arm. "Why not? Why can you not be pregnant? All signs point to it. You've not had your monthly. You are experiencing morning sickness, and your urine shows signs of pregnancy. What more do you need, my friend?"

Ornella shook her head. "But I'm too old to be pregnant."

Ramona chuckled. "Apparently not." The midwife sat down next to her and gently took both her hands. "Ornella, you may be older than most pregnant women, but you are healthier and stronger than most women your age. You've borne four healthy children. Children I delivered myself. You are a sturdy woman."

Ornella shook her head as another wave of nausea swept over her. As hard as she tried, she couldn't deny the symptoms. Her body screamed. "Pregnant! Pregnant! Pregnant!"

She buried her face in her hands. All her dreams of freedom, of painting, and of opening an art gallery suddenly vanished. What lay ahead was nothing but a life of caring for another infant at a time in her life when she was tired of raising infants. Wasn't it time to care for herself for once?

Her face grew warm as guilt washed over her. What kind of woman was she? How could she be so selfish? Yet, was it selfish to want to do something for oneself?

The needs of her unborn child and her own needs swirled inside her in a wild, tornadic dance, pulling her in two opposite directions at once. Ripping her already fragmented soul into shreds of agonizing conflict.

Like a tsunami, wave after wave of darkness

overwhelmed her, drowning every last vestige of hope. Her future crashed before her very eyes, leaving in its wake a pile of emotional rubble that buried her every dream. Her well-planned life had fallen apart, leaving her only the bitter ashes of regret.

Ornella closed her eyes and took in a deep breath to ease the tightness in her chest. There was nothing she could do but accept the truth. What was done was done. There was only one way to go and that was forward. But how?

"Ornella?" Ramona's voice called to her like a distant echo. "Ornella, look at me." Ramona patted her hand.

Slowly, Ornella looked up. The midwife's face blurred through the hot tears that stung Ornella's eyes.

"This news is not the end of the world, Ornella. Trust God. It is by His will that you are with child. He has a plan."

Trust in the Lord. Clarissa's words surfaced from the depths of Ornella's soul. *Lean not to your own understanding.* Why did the voice of her own understanding squelch the voice of the Lord? *He has a plan.* A plan that was not her plan. Her muscles stiffened. Had she no right at all to her own plans? Must she forever sacrifice her own plan for God's plan?

She lowered her voice. "Ramona, thank you for your encouragement. I am so distraught, I can't think straight. I need to go home and talk with Francesco."

Ornella sighed. How would Francesco receive the

news? Would he be happy? Shocked? Distressed? He was worried enough about the strike and its threat to their livelihood without adding to that the weight of another mouth to feed. When he heard the news, what would he say?

Ornella blinked back the hot tears that flooded her eyes. If she were brutally honest with herself, she did not want this pregnancy. She did not want another child. She already had four children. Four was the perfect number for her. The number she'd always wanted. The number she'd planned for. She didn't need another child. She already had the perfect family. Two boys. Two girls. Another child would destroy the perfect balance.

Heat rose to her face. How could she, a Christian woman, think such foolish thoughts? How could she resent the arrival of an innocent child into her life? Especially the child in her own womb? What kind of woman was she to blame an innocent, tiny baby for intruding into her life? What kind of selfish monster was she to reject her own child?

"Ornella. Ornella." Ramona's kind voice pierced Ornella's consciousness. "Many women are shocked by the news of an unexpected pregnancy but live to rejoice in it once they hold their precious child in their arms. You will do the same. You will see." Ramona smiled. "Besides, you now have four older children to help you."

Ornella lifted her gaze toward Ramona. Over the past several years, the middle-aged woman had served not only as her midwife but had also become a close friend. "I hope you're right." But despite Ramona's words, Ornella could not see how an unexpected and an unwanted child could bring rejoicing.

Ramona smiled. "God made us women to bear life. Life, Ornella. What a great privilege it is to be able to co-create with the God of the universe! Fix your mind on that."

But the only thing Ornella could fix her mind on was that her life had suddenly and without warning been turned upside down. All of her well-thought-out plans had now been ruined.

Ramona gave her a hug. "Children are a gift from the Lord, Ornella. Never forget that."

While Ramona was right, it wasn't *she* who was expecting a child in middle-age.

Ornella rose, her head spinning with the shock of it all. The news had knocked her off her feet. But she had to get up. She had to remain strong. She had to make the best of things. For Francesco's sake. For her children's sake. And for the sake of the child to come.

As for her own sake?

That was a matter she would have to push aside yet again.

FRIDAY, June 22, 1877

. . .

INSTEAD OF GOING STRAIGHT HOME after leaving the midwife, Ornella went to the fields to give Francesco the news. Her heart pounded within her at the expectation of his response. What would he say? How would he react? Would he be happy or sad?

She found him in the tomato fields, tending to preparations for the first tomato harvest in July. Her heart went out to him as he bent over the growing plants in the sun's scorching heat. Although it was not yet noon, the day had already grown hot and humid.

As she approached him, several farmhands working at his side looked up. William called out to him with a signature smile. "Francesco, your bride is here."

Upon hearing William's words, Francesco drew away from the men, a look of alarm on his face. He ran toward her. "Ornella, what are you doing here? Is everything all right?"

Nodding, she choked back the tears. "I need to talk with you."

His face turning pale, he took her gently by the arm. "Come. Let's go sit under the oak tree where we can talk privately."

Ornella accompanied him to a centuries-old oak tree, a short distance from the tomato fields. They sat down on a clump of soft grass outside earshot of the farmhands.

"Francesco." Tears flowed from Ornella's eyes.

Twitches of panic gripped his face as he waited patiently for her to speak.

She forced the difficult words lodged in her throat to come to the surface. "We are going to have another child."

He released a long sigh of relief and laughed. "Thank God. That is wonderful news, Ornella." He took her hands. "I thought you were going to tell me that something terrible had happened to one of the children." He drew her into his arms and embraced her. "From the look on your face, I didn't know what to think."

Another flood of tears erupted from her soul. "But, Francesco. We can't afford another child. Especially not now, with the strike going on."

His eyes locked onto hers as he spoke in a calm, measured tone. "Ornella, God will provide for all of our needs. It is His promise to His children."

She nodded and lowered her eyes. "Yes. I must trust God to provide. But, truth be told, it's more than that."

He lifted her chin. "What is it, dearest one?"

"I can hardly say it, I am so ashamed." Heat seeped into her cheeks as she struggled to speak the awful words. "Francesco, I don't want this child."

A pained look crossed his face. He stroked her cheek. "You are simply upset by the disruption in your plans." He pushed back a stray tendril from her forehead. "But

God has other plans, Ornella. Far better than our own. We must yield to them."

Although her heart told her Francesco was right, her mind did not want to face that truth. Especially not now that she was within reach of her dream. That she could taste it and touch it. Why would God put an obstacle in her way at this precise moment in time when everything was going just the way she'd planned?

"Francesco, this is not the first time I have put aside my dream for you and our children. Will there ever come a time that is *my* time? "

He stroked her hair but remained silent.

She sniffed back tears. "I know I come across as very selfish. I don't mean to. It's just that I've spent my whole life fulfilling the needs of my family. Now I would like to spend some time fulfilling my own needs for a change."

'I understand, Ornella. But having another child doesn't mean you will never be able to pursue your art. You can set aside time to paint while the baby is asleep. Or Teresa can take care of the child for a couple of hours. There are ways to overcome such obstacles. It's all about how we look at them."

"I know that what you are saying is true. But I am in a state of shock at the unexpected news."

"I am as well." He smiled and squeezed her hand.

But despite Francesco's encouragement, Ornella still didn't like the idea of having to spend the next several years raising another child. Years she'd planned to devote to herself and her own dreams.

She glanced beyond him toward the farmhands. If the strike continued, they would have to let the men go. What would happen then? How would they feed five children instead of four?

She returned her gaze to her husband. "With the strike getting worse, how will we provide for another child?"

Francesco smiled. "God will supply all that we need, my dearest. You must not worry."

His strength soothed the innermost depths of her soul. "I was so afraid you'd be upset at the news."

Francesco tenderly lifted her chin and looked deep into her eyes. "Ornella, does not the Bible tell us that children are a reward from the Lord? And happy is the man whose quiver is full of them?" He chuckled. "A quiver is five. We now will have a quiver."

"Yes, but the Bible says happy is the *man* whose quiver is full of them, not the woman."

Francesco laughed. "I think the verse could apply to both the man and the woman."

But Ornella wasn't so sure. While she was happy for Francesco, she was not happy for herself. It fell to the woman to bear the brunt of child-rearing. Not only did the woman have to go through the trials and discomfort of carrying the child for nine months and then endure the agonizing birth pains, but she also had to manage firsthand the problems of rearing the children. And it was the woman who had to postpone her personal dreams, not the man. The man could continue in his normal pursuits, whatever those might look like. The woman could not.

He squared his gaze on hers. "What is really troubling you, Ornella?" His voice carried an impatient edge to it.

She returned his steadied gaze. "The news of this pregnancy has ripped my soul in two, Francesco. Before I learned of the pregnancy, I was heading in the direction of my dream. I had a clear path before me. A clear sense of purpose and the freedom to accomplish that purpose. I even found the perfect location to rent for my art gallery. But now I am being pulled in the opposite direction, away from my dream. I've been forced into a purpose and a path I don't want. And I don't know how to reconcile the two, or if it is even possible. I must give up one in order to have the other. And now that I am pregnant, I have no choice."

Francesco shook his head, a puzzled look on his face. "I'm trying hard to understand, Ornella. Why must you give up one in order to have the other? Can you not join the two paths?

"But how, Francesco? If I must remain home to raise a baby, how can I open an art gallery that will require my presence and time?"

"Perhaps it is only a matter of postponing your dream for the time being."

She stiffened. "But that's what I've been doing all these years. Postponing my dream for the sake of others. How long must I do this? I am approaching fifty years of age. How many more years do I have left?"

He took her hand. "Perhaps the Lord is asking you to sacrifice your dream for the sake of the child within you?"

Her soul exploded within her. Impossible! It took all of her self-control to keep from uttering words she would later regret. "Why would God give me a dream only to ask me to give it up?"

Francesco tunneled his fingers through his hair. "God asked Abraham to sacrifice Isaac."

"Yes, but God also restored Isaac to Abraham."

"What if the Lord is asking you to give up your dream only to restore it to you at a later time? What if He is presenting you with an Isaac experience?"

Francesco's words struck a chord deep within her. Was God testing her to show her what was truly in her heart?

He caressed her hand. "Ornella, your first responsibility is toward your family. We have children who need to be cared for."

Her chest tightened. "Don't you think I know that?" Her fists clenched. The woman paid the greater price for having children. Yes, the man had to work hard to support the family, but it fell to the woman to carry the greater part of the load. How would Francesco feel if their roles were reversed?

She swallowed hard, in a vain attempt to keep bitterness from taking root in her heart.

"Ornella dearest, we are in this together. We are husband and wife. We share everything, both the joys of life and its sorrows."

"Yes, that is true, Francesco. But we do not share the same actual burdens. I am the one who is carrying the child in my body and feeling the physical discomfort. I am the one who will have to go through the pain of childbirth. I am the one who will be raising the child. I am the one who must postpone my dreams yet again. You continue to do what you've always done." She averted her eyes. "It just doesn't seem fair."

Annoyance filled his eyes. "Well, then, that is something you must take up with God. He designed things that way. The woman is to carry the child while the man works to support both the mother and the child. We both have an important role to play."

But why did she not feel this way? Why did it seem that the woman gave more in a marriage than the man? Why was the man admired for following his dream but the woman was not? Why did society not expect that a man should find complete fulfillment in fatherhood alone, while that same society expected a woman to find complete fulfillment in motherhood alone? Ornella bristled at the injustice of it all. That's easy for you to say. You aren't being asked to give up your dream of farming."

Francesco shook his head in frustration. "Farming is not my dream, Ornella. It is my job. My dream is to make you happy."

"But, admit it, Francesco. Farming has been your dream ever since you were a little boy and used to work at your father's side in the field. You've told me that many times. And you've achieved your dream." She swallowed the bile that rose to her throat. "Well, I have a dream, too. My dream is art. Why must I be prevented from achieving my dream simply because I am a woman? Isn't that unjust?"

He squared his jaw. "I don't know what to say."

There was nothing more to say. Francesco was too much entrenched in their patriarchal Italian culture to be willing to see things in a different light. He expected her to follow tradition. To put her dream aside in order to take care of their family.

She choked back a cry. Her lot had been cast. Now she had a choice. She could either be miserable for the rest of her life, or she could find another way to fulfill her dream.

Knowing she had a choice gave her some semblance of control. Determination pulsed within her. No matter what Francesco said, she would find a way to fulfill her dream.

Although he worked hard for the family, he was still living his dream. Surely, it wasn't easy to work in the fields as he did, no matter what the weather. How often had she witnessed his return after a sudden downpour, cold and soaked to the bone? How often had he gone out to the barn in the dead of winter and repaired farm equipment with no heat to keep him warm? Several times he'd come close to experiencing hypothermia.

Yet, he was still following his dream.

What was life without a dream? What was a human being without a dream? As good as dead. If she did not pursue her dream, she would die on the inside. Why couldn't Francesco understand that? Why couldn't men in general understand that? Why did they expect that a woman should be content simply running a home and raising children? It didn't make sense. Even women in the Bible conducted business outside the home. Deborah. Lydia. The woman of Proverbs 31.

A war raged inside her. A war between the past and the future. Between tradition and progress. Between desire and duty.

Ornella shook her head. Women had to work harder than men to achieve the same goals. Women had to prove themselves in ways that men did not. Yet, there were those of her female artist peers who had begun to protest against the injustice as well. And not only protest against it. They had done something about it. Having been refused admission into art schools, these female artists had discovered alternative ways to study art through private lessons or self-study. Perhaps Ornella could do the same.

But how with a new baby on the way?

"Ornella, look at me." Francesco's gentle voice drew her back from her mental meanderings to the present moment. "What you need is a few days of good rest. Rest will give you a fresh and more realistic perspective on life."

"Rest?" She came close to laughing in his face. "Francesco, you must be joking. How can I take a few days of rest? Who will cook, clean, and tend to the children? My mother is becoming more fragile day by day. She can do only such much to help me."

"But we have older children now. Teresa is fourteen, almost a grown woman herself. And Caterina is not far behind. Now is the time to enlist more of their help. They must learn that, as members of our family, they are required to contribute to the best of their ability."

Ornella nodded. "And our sons as well." She sighed. "I think we've been raising them with the mentality that household chores are woman's work." She knit her brows together. "We women aren't on this earth simply to pick up after our men." An unusual sharpness edged her voice.

Francesco looked into her eyes. "Ornella, where is this bitterness coming from? It is unlike you to talk like this."

She lowered her eyes. "I don't know, Francesco. Perhaps it's that I've pent up my true feelings for so long that only now are they erupting." She looked up at him. "Sometimes I feel as though I've been living a lie. I have pretended for far too long that marriage and motherhood are enough for me. But I can no longer pretend. I can no longer lie to myself nor to anyone else. Marriage and motherhood are not enough for me. Why is it expected that a man should not be satisfied with marriage and fatherhood alone while a woman should be?" She shook her head. "No, Francesco. I must follow the dream God gave me to become an artist. If I don't, I will die."

Confusion lined his face. He gently stroked her hair. "Whatever you do, do not allow a root of bitterness to spring up within you, Ornella. It will only end up harming you."

"I know, Francesco. I'm trying not to be bitter. Please pray for me."

"I will, darling." He planted a kiss on her forehead. "Tonight at dinner, when I give the children the news, I will explain to them that when the new baby arrives, we will need their help more than ever before."

His words brought Ornella some relief. Pressing his hand to her face, she closed her eyes tight, squeezing the hot tears onto her cheeks. "I love you so very much, Francesco."

"And I, you, Ornella. Do not worry, and do not be afraid. The Lord will provide everything we need." He wiped a tear from her cheek. "And He will make a way for you to pursue your passion for art."

She nodded. "I hope you're right. It's just that I'm having trouble sorting out my feelings. I didn't feel this way about our other children. I suppose it's that I was younger then. The hope of having enough time to fulfill my dream sustained me. But now that I am older, my remaining time on this earth seems far less. And I am tired now. I don't know if I will have the strength to raise another child."

"I understand, dearest." He pushed a stray tendril behind her ear. "But this pregnancy is no surprise to God."

She looked toward the tomato fields, now laden with ripening fruit. The sun beat down on the men bent over the growing plants as they measured the status of the crop for harvest. "I should be going. You have to get back to work, and I need to get home. I'll break the news to Mama. Tonight we can tell the children at dinner."

His face beamed. "I have a hunch they will be overjoyed." He took her by the hand and helped her up from their place on the grass. "This child will be a great blessing to all of us, Ornella. Rest in that truth."

She nodded half-heartedly. "I hope you're right." Yes, every child should be a blessing. But this pregnancy was different from her four previous pregnancies. Why? An ominous shudder ran through her as she embraced Francesco. "I'll see you this evening."

"I wish I could go home with you now." He looked deep into her eyes. "Be careful as you walk home."

She kissed his cheek. "I will." She bade him farewell and made her way back to the farmhouse. Her next order of business was to break the news to Mama.

CHAPTER
SIX

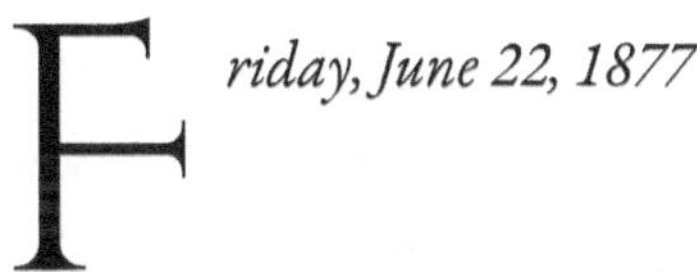

riday, June 22, 1877

FRANCESCO SHOVED his hands into his pockets as his gaze followed Ornella's departure. To protect her from further worry, he'd kept his concerns about the baby to himself. Although he loved children, the thought of a new mouth to feed in their current financial circumstances and at their advanced ages stirred deep consternation in his soul. He was already two years over the half-century mark, and Ornella was fast approaching it. To have a new baby at an age when they should be grandparenting instead deeply troubled him.

That Ornella was unhappy about the pregnancy

bothered him as well. He'd never seen her like this. And the bitterness that pervaded her demeanor was so contrary to her usual contented spirit. While he understood her passion for art, he had difficulty grasping the reason she thought another child would interfere with her dream. As the baby grew, would she not have more time to pursue what she loved?

He turned back toward the fields and toward the concerns of his farm. Concerns that ate at the pit of his stomach. The railroad strike was now in full swing, with violence breaking out in Philadelphia as well as in Baltimore and Pittsburgh. Two rioters had been killed, and there was fear that more would die. Confusion reigned as the strike spread not only eastward but also westward toward Chicago and St. Louis.

Locally, the Pennsylvania Railroad had canceled runs between Philadelphia and Cape May. Reports had reached him that strikers had prevented trains from leaving the stations. Even men from Cape May who worked on the Pennsylvania Railroad were involved, and they'd been stirring up strife in the area, attempting through various ethical and unethical means to persuade farm workers and fishermen to support the strike. Tensions had mounted and had reached dangerous levels. Things did not look good.

Upon seeing Ornella's worried frame of mind, Francesco had kept this news from her. She was already upset enough about the pregnancy without his adding to her distress.

He wiped a palm across his sweaty face and let out a long breath. Summer in New Jersey could be overwhelming with its excessive heat and humidity. And when one had to spend the entire day working in the hot sun, it was even more overwhelming.

A gunshot blast in the distance stopped him short, thrusting his heart into a tailspin. For a terrifying instant he froze, the blood in his veins turning to ice. From what direction had the shot come? Was Ornella safe? And what about his men?

He bolted across the field just as William ran toward him.

"Francesco! Come quickly! Mino has been shot." Mino was Francesco's right-hand man, a longtime employee and father of seven children. He'd refused to support the local strikers, choosing instead to remain on the job to provide for his family and to express his loyalty to Francesco.

Francesco's breath caught in his throat. "Is he still alive?"

William nodded emphatically. "Thank the good Lawd, yes. But he be losin' blood fast. The bullet put a hole in his leg, and he be needin' a doctor right away."

Francesco ran alongside William, panting in the heavy, humid air. "What happened?"

"Tomás lost his temper because Mino refused to support the local strikers."

Francesco's heart plummeted to his feet. Ever since Tomás had started working on the farm, he'd been a trouble-maker. Francesco should never have hired him, but compassion for the man's desperate financial situation had prompted him to offer Tomàs a job. A decision Francesco now deeply regretted.

He let out a frustrated sigh. He had enough worries just trying to raise and sell crops without having to contend with political issues, too. The strike upheaval was now affecting not only the farm's economy but also the relationship among the workers. For the past several days, it had stirred tension among them, dividing them almost equally between those who wanted to support the local strikers and those who did not. Interestingly, the locally-based railroad workers who supported the strike were mostly single men without families, while those who opposed the strike were married men with wives and children.

Struggling to catch his breath in the intense heat, Francesco turned toward William. "We need to get Mino to Dr. Gerken right away."

"Alex has already gone to the barn to fetch the horse and wagon."

Oh, God! Spare Mino's life! Francesco prayed silently as he ran alongside William toward the group of farmhands huddled over a bleeding Mino.

Francesco pushed through the group of men, his eyes settling on his wounded friend and employee. Two of the men had placed Mino on a makeshift stretcher. One of the workers had used a handkerchief to create a tourniquet around Mino's leg to stop the bleeding, but the handkerchief was already soaked through with blood.

Francesco placed a hand on Mino's arm. "Mino, my friend, I'm so sorry this happened."

Mino dipped his chin. His face was pale as blood oozed through the tourniquet on his leg. He struggled to speak. "Please send word to my wife." His voice quivering, his intense gaze met Francesco's eyes. "And tell her I love her."

A lump formed in Francesco's throat. Did Mino sense he would die? "I will, my friend. May God be with you." Francesco turned to William. "Where is the wagon?"

No sooner had he asked the question than Alex Billings drove up with the horse and wagon. In a few moments, the men had lifted Mino onto the wagon and carried him away toward Dr. Gerken's office, about two miles away.

Although Francesco wanted to go with them, he decided against it. Given the strife among the other men, it would be too dangerous to leave them behind. Who knew what could happen? Tensions were high, and he could not afford another outburst. Whatever he had to do, he would keep the peace.

He released a long breath. "We need to notify Mino's wife of his injury."

William again was quick to reply. "I've already sent word. She be on her way to the doctor's office."

His heart heavy with grief, Francesco sat down on a nearby log, motioning William to join him. "Tell me everything that happened."

William sat down next to him and proceeded to recount the details of the incident. "Tomás started mocking Mino for refusin' to participate in the strike. When Mino kept on refusin' to engage him, Tomás flew into a rage, pulled out a revolver from his trousers, and shot him."

Francesco shook his head, intense regret at hiring Tomás flooding his soul yet again. "Where is Tomás now?"

"He took off before we could subdue him. Who knows where he be?"

"Have you called the police?"

William smiled and placed a hand on Francesco's forearm. "Done as well. I sent Eddie Fuller into town to the sheriff's office to file a report."

Francesco turned toward his friend and gave him an approving smile. "I need to promote you to senior foreman."

William chuckled. "That be soundin' like a good idea to me."

Francesco gazed into the distance. "I thank God that

Mino wasn't killed. Although the situation is bad enough as it is, we would have had a real mess on our hands then."

William nodded. 'No tellin' what those strikers will do once they gets their heads in a tizzy. Like the Good Book say, '*The wrath of man worketh not the righteousness of God*.'"

Francesco sighed. "Amen to that."

William picked up a twig and started peeling off the bark. "Do you think the strike will end soon?"

"I hope so." Francesco paused. "For a lot of reasons." Not the least of which was the imminent birth of his new child. Truth be told, it wasn't the best time to welcome a new baby to the family. But was there ever a best time?

William peeled the last bit of bark off the twig. "I saw Ornella in the fields earlier. Thank God she missed the shootin'."

A shiver ran through Francesco. He took in a long, deep breath. "Yes. Thank God." His voice was barely a whisper. He turned toward William. "She's with child."

Raising both eyebrows, William breathed out a low whistle. "Thank God twice then."

Francesco shuddered at the thought that, had Ornella been in the line of fire, both she and their child could have been killed.

He swallowed hard. He would hold Ornella extra close to his heart later that night.

Friday, June 22, 1877

Upon arriving home from the fields, Ornella found Mama in the kitchen removing two loaves of homemade bread from the oven. The fragrant, yeasty aroma filled the air, soothing Ornella's troubled soul.

"*Ciao*, Mama. I'm glad to see you're up. You must be feeling better."

Mama placed the two loaves of piping hot bread on the cast iron stovetop and closed the oven door. "Thank the good Lord, I am." She smiled. "In fact, I felt so good that I thought I'd bake us some bread for dinner."

"Thank you. That was thoughtful of you."

Mama stopped and studied her daughter's face. "Something's troubling you." Mama was an astute woman. Ever since Ornella was a little girl, her mother always knew when something was wrong. And now, Ornella felt like that little girl again. "I have something very important to tell you, Mama."

Mama placed the potholders on the kitchen table. "Let's go sit in the parlor. The children are outside playing. We can talk privately."

Ornella followed her mother into the parlor and sat down on the sofa next to her.

Mama took both her hands. "What is it, *figlia mia*?

Tears flooded Ornella's eyes. When Mama called her *my daughter*, Ornella always pictured herself as the little girl who'd skinned her knee and then went to her mother for a kiss of comfort.

Ornella drew in a deep breath. "Mama, I'm pregnant."

Mama's eyes widened into huge orbs, while her lips spanned the distance between her ears. "Praise be to God!" She drew Ornella toward her and engulfed her in a tight hug.

After a long moment, Ornella pulled back. "But, Mama, do you understand what this means?"

Mama laughed. "It means I'm going to have another grandchild."

Of course Mama could be happy. She wasn't the one who would carry the child, give birth to the child, and raise the child. "But I'm too old to have a baby. I'm almost fifty. That's half a century, Mama."

Mama chuckled. "I know that you are almost fifty years old." She rubbed Ornella's hand. "Think of it this way. A baby will keep you young."

"But I'm tired of raising children. I want to be free to paint and to open my art gallery."

"Now, now, dearest one. Having another child doesn't mean you won't be able to do those things."

"But when, Mama? By the time this child is grown, I will be nearly seventy years old." The thought shook her. "If I live that long." She turned her gaze toward Mama.

"And if I don't, I won't ever get to fulfill any of my own dreams."

"Who says that children should keep a woman from fulfilling her dreams?" Mama's eyes took on a wistful look.

Mama's words took Ornella by surprise. "But how can I open an art gallery with a new baby?"

Mama gave her a knowing smile. "How can you not?"

Ornella's breath caught. "Mama, I never thought I'd live to hear you say such a thing. You yourself gave up your dream of singing with the opera."

Mama locked her gaze onto Ornella's. "I know now that I did not have to give up my dream. I only thought I did."

Ornella's breath caught. "Mama, what are you saying?"

"I'm saying that nothing should keep a woman from fulling her dream. Neither children, nor marriage, nor any other human being, nor any situation. If her dream is from God and is strong enough, a woman will find a way to achieve it."

Mama's surprising words left Ornella stunned. Had dreams resided in the hearts of the women of mama's generation as well? Had those women been too afraid to challenge the *status quo*? Had they been stifled by the society in which they lived?

She studied Mama's face. "But what about obstacles

that come against a woman's dream and create conflict within her to the point that she must choose one path over the other? Like the responsibilities of raising children that have kept me bound to the home for so many years?"

Mama's gaze grew pensive. "Only a force more powerful than the dream can stifle the dream." Her eyes were tender pools of love. "And you alone are the one who determines if you will allow your dream to be stifled." Mama stroked her hand. "Remember this, *figlia mia*. Obstacles are servants of the dream. A strong-enough dream will overcome any obstacle standing in its way."

Ornella pondered Mama's words.

Mama leaned forward. "*Figlia mia*, our talents are given to us by God to implement our dream. We must not bury those talents, just as we must not bury the dream. To bury one's dream is to bury one's soul."

To bury one's soul. That's what had happened to Ornella. For far too long, she had buried her dream. And in so doing, she had buried her soul. It was now time to resurrect it. But how?

"I've buried my dream for a long time, Mama."

'Then you must take it up and never put it down again."

"But how, Mama, without hurting Francesco and the children?"

"You are hurting them by not pursuing your dream.

You are taking out on them the frustration of your failure to be true to yourself."

Mama's words were like a lightning bolt of truth penetrating Ornella's heart. "I've been afraid. I've been torn between my family and my art."

"Mama patted her hand. "Life does not have to be either-or, my dear Ornella. It can be both-and. There is a way to make it so. You simply have to find that way. And with God's help, you will."

Ornella studied Mama's eyes. Her words came from a place of deep pain where wisdom had blossomed amid the thorns of profound heartache. The heartache Mama had endured from burying her own dream.

"Sometimes I feel trapped in motherhood, Mama. Sometimes I just want to be free of the burdens."

"Freedom comes from within, my child. It is not dependent on our external circumstances nor our surroundings. You can be free with a dozen children and a prisoner with none."

But Ornella wasn't so sure.

Mama's gaze locked onto hers. "What is it you really want, Ornella?"

Ornella searched her soul. "What I really want is for my life to go according to my plans. I've never liked surprises."

Mama chuckled. "What life turns out as one plans, my dear daughter? In the end, God has His own plan for each of our lives, and that is always the best plan."

"Then are we merely puppets in the hands of an almighty God?" Just uttering the words aroused the fear of the Lord in Ornella's soul.

"We have a free will, dear one. We can choose to align ourselves with God's plan for our lives, or we can choose to go our own way and follow our own plans. But we must understand that to follow our own plans will mean destruction for us in the end."

"But what is God's plan for me, Mama? I don't even know."

"Well, being a wife and mother is obviously part of His plan for you. But being an artist is also part of His plan. Why would God have given you a passion and talent for art if He did not want you to create art for Him?"

"I don't know how to do both at the same time. The demands of motherhood overwhelm me."

"Life occurs in phases, Ornella. Especially for a woman. At times the phases overlap. At other times, they do not."

Confusion swirled around in Ornella's mind, churning up a whirlwind of tormenting emotions. Foremost among them was fear. Truth be told, she was afraid of what the future held for a middle-aged woman about to have a baby. Would she survive the delivery? Would there be enough money to support another child? Would she be able to pursue her love of art?

And then, to her surprise, there was anger. Why was

she angry? And at whom? At Francesco? At God? It wasn't as if they'd both conspired against her. Yet, why did she feel this way? Certainly she'd had a part in this pregnancy as well.

Guilt washed over her. What kind of a woman was she? She should be happy, shouldn't she? Yet, she was far from happy. She was miserable.

She leaned forward and buried her face in Mama's chest. "Oh, Mama. I'm such a terrible person. What am I going to do?"

"You're going to bear a beautiful child whom you will love with all your heart. A child who will bring you great joy and show you the heart of God."

Why did Mama's words sound ominous instead of comforting? Ornella already had four children whom she loved with all her heart. They'd already shown her the heart of God. She didn't need another child to show her His heart. "I hope you're right, Mama."

Mama stroked her cheek. "Now then. Decide to enjoy this pregnancy. It will very likely be your last."

Ornella raised her head and gave Mama a slanted look. "That's what I thought about the fourth one."

The sound of chatter in the next room interrupted their conversation. "I'd better go tend to the children." She looked at Mama. "Please don't say anything to them just yet. Francesco wants to give them the news at dinner tonight."

"Don't worry. I won't say a word."

Before Ornella could get up to greet them, the children rushed into the parlor toward her. "Mama! Mama! The carnival is coming to town!"

Ornella tensed. She did not need this right now. "You know how I feel about carnivals. They are dens of sin."

"But, Mama!" Caterina raised her voice in protest. "There are some good parts. Like the merry-go-round and the cotton candy."

"And the elephants and camels." For once, Marco agreed with his older sister. "Please, Mama, please let us go."

The children's request irritated Ornella. With everything else she had on her mind, this was not the time for them to discuss the carnival. "I'll talk with your father about it later. For now, get your homework done before dinner."

To her great relief, this time the children obeyed her without another word.

SEVEN

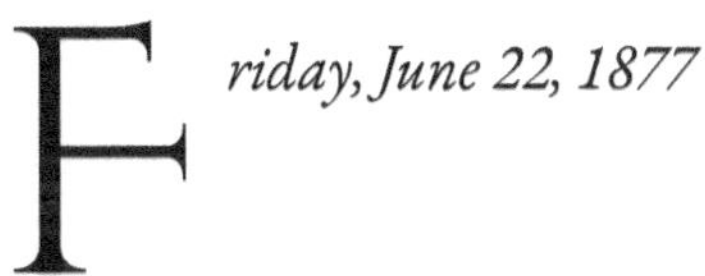

Friday, June 22, 1877

THAT NIGHT, Francesco returned home heavy-laden. Whereas Ornella's news about their forthcoming baby should have been foremost in his mind, the shooting incident on the farm consumed his thoughts instead.

A huge rift had erupted among the farmhands, with some promoting the strike and others protesting it. Worst of all, Mino was in critical condition and might not make it through the night. Upon receiving the news, his wife Yolanda had succumbed to hysteria. Not to mention, the police had come to the farm to begin investigations regarding the whereabouts of Tomás.

Burdened to the limit, Francesco entered the farmhouse through the back door and found Ornella preparing the evening meal.

"Francesco." She hurried to him and gave him a warm embrace.

He slid his hands down her arms. "I have some tragic news."

Her pulse rising, Ornella searched his eyes. "What tragic news?"

"A shooting occurred on the farm shortly after you left."

Ornella gasped as her hand flew to her mouth. "Oh, no! What happened?"

"It had to do with the strike. There is division among the men. When Mino refused to support the local railroad strikers, Tomás grew violent and shot him in the leg. Mino lost a lot of blood. The men rushed him to Dr. Gerken's office. He is in serious condition and not expected to live through the night."

Ornella lowered herself slowly into a chair. "Dear God, help us." She looked up at her husband. "Is there anything I can do?"

"Perhaps you can bring a meal to Yolanda and her children tomorrow. She is with Mino now and is beside herself with worry."

Francesco sat down in a chair next to Ornella. "I'm so sorry to bring this bad news on the same day we received such good news about the baby."

Ornella lifted tear-filled eyes toward him. "Francesco, why do I not believe that the news about the baby is good?"

He placed his hand under her chin and lifted it, looking squarely into her eyes. Those beautiful, dark eyes that had forever captured his heart so many years before. "You are tired, dearest one. The thought of even more work overwhelms you."

She leaned her face into his palm, tears trickling down her cheeks as she closed her eyes. "It is more than that, Francesco. This pregnancy seems different. For the first time, I am afraid."

"Afraid of what, dearest?"

"I don't know exactly. I'm eight years older than I was when I had Marco. What if I don't survive? What if I die and leave our children motherless? What if our baby dies?"

Panic flitted through him, but he quickly dismissed it. The thought of losing Ornella was more than he could bear. He caressed her cheek. "You worry about so many things, Ornella. And the things you worry about rarely, if ever, come to pass. Now be at peace. Our feelings can betray us. Only God's Word speaks truth. And God's Word commands us to be anxious for nothing, but to give thanks in everything. So we will resist anxiety in the Name of our Lord Jesus, and we will give thanks for this new child He has seen fit to give us. Children are a gift from His hand. We will accept this child as His gift."

Before Ornella could respond, Marco's sudden shout interrupted the conversation. "Papa! Papa!" His son rushed up to Francesco and gave him a hug. "Can we go to the carnival?"

"The carnival?" Francesco embraced his youngest child. The one he and Ornella had thought would be their last.

"Yes. Papa. The carnival is coming to Cape May, and Caterina and I want to go."

Francesco cast a questioning look at Ornella.

"I told them they could discuss it with you later."

Marco drew closer, his dark eyes pleading. "It's later now, Papa."

"Marco, I think we should save this conversation until after dinner. Meanwhile, how was your day, my son?"

He jutted his chin. "Awful." Scowling, he pointed to his sister who had followed him into the kitchen. "Caterina and I had an argument."

Francesco quirked an eyebrow. "Over what?"

"Over who would get to feed Sofia."

"And who finally fed Sofia?"

Marco lowered his eyes. "She didn't get fed."

Francesco drew back, widened his eyes, and held Marco at arm's length. "So the kitten is now hungry because of you and Caterina?"

"It's Caterina's fault, Papa." Marco pointed to

Caterina who was standing a few feet away. "She wouldn't let me feed her."

Papa motioned to his daughter to come closer. "Caterina, what do you have to say for yourself? Why would you not let your brother feed the kitten?"

"Because I didn't think he knew how."

Marco stomped his foot and, drawing his eyebrows together in a straight line, folded his arms across his chest. "I do so know how to feed the kitten."

"Now, now, children. I think this nonsense needs to stop, don't you?" Papa turned to Caterina. "Marco is eight years old. He is old enough to feed the kitten. So I think you can give him a turn once in a while." He glanced at Marco. "Besides, as I understand it, the kitten is *his* pet, isn't she?"

"Yes, Papa. But Marco can't have the kitten all to himself. It's not fair. He could share her with me."

Papa's eyebrows met his hairline. "Ah, now I see the real reason for the argument. Do you see it, Caterina?"

She shook her head.

"I think the real reason is rivalry between you and your little brother. You are jealous that he has a pet and you don't."

Caterina blushed.

"Am I right, Caterina?"

She nodded but did not say a word.

He turned to Marco. "Do you think you could share Sofia with Caterina?"

Marco hesitated, his face in a pout. "I guess so. I could feed Sofia in the morning and Caterina could feed her at night."

Papa smiled. "That sounds like a good compromise to me." He turned toward Ornella. "What do you think?"

"I think it's an excellent compromise."

Caterina pursed her lips and glared at Marco. "You always get me into trouble."

Papa gave her a stern look. "Caterina, no one gets us into trouble. We get ourselves into trouble. Now enough of this silliness. It's time to feed Sofia and then to sit down at the table to eat."

After a surprisingly peaceful dinner, Francesco called for his children's attention. "Children, I need you all to be as quiet as you can. I have some very exciting news to share."

"I know! The strike is over." Giovanni shouted from the far end of the table.

The painful memory of the day's tragedy struck Francesco yet again. Swallowing hard, he shook his head. "No, Giovanni. The strike is still on, but I have far better news."

"I know! I know, Papa!" Marco sat on the edge of his chair. "You're going to let us get a puppy."

Francesco smiled. "Why would you want a puppy now that you have a kitten?"

"Because puppies are more fun."

"No they're not." Caterina slid in on Marco's verbal coattails. "Kittens are more fun."

Francesco sighed. "Children, enough of the bickering. The news I have is even better than a new puppy."

"What can be better than a puppy?" Marco insisted.

Fourteen-year-old Teresa broke into a wide grin. "I know. We're going to have a new baby in the family."

Francesco laughed aloud. "You are right, Teresa, and very perceptive, I might add. God has given us a new little Lombardi."

Cheering wildly, the children clapped their hands. All except for Marco.

Papa quirked an eyebrow. "Aren't you excited about the news, Marco?"'

"No. Now I'll have to share Sofia with the new baby, too."

Francesco fixed his gaze on Marco. "I see. I suppose you could work out another compromise, don't you think?"

Marco lowered his eyes. "I guess so."

Caterina wiggled in her chair. "When will the baby come, Papa?"

"It looks as though our new little one will arrive sometime around Christmas."

"Christmas?" Giovanni shouted. "We have to make sure we buy him a present."

"What makes you think it will be a boy?" Teresa teased.

"Of course it will be a boy." Giovanni gave her a proud look.

Papa intervened. "Only God knows those things, Giovanni. We will be happy and thankful for whoever God sends us."

"I want another sister," Caterina exclaimed. "Little brothers are nothing but pests." She glared at Marco who stuck his tongue out at her.

Papa gave the children a stern look. "Now, now, children. Let's be kind to one another and remain unified. We have much to do to prepare for our new family member."

"Yes, children." Ornella was quick to agree. "I will need much help to prepare for the baby, and especially after the baby arrives. Now that you are all growing older, I will expect more from you."

"I'll give the baby a bath," Teresa said.

"And I'll take the baby out for a walk in the baby carriage," Giovanni offered.

Papa smiled. "And who will volunteer to change the baby's diapers?"

No one responded.

Papa laughed and looked at Ornella. "Well, I suppose we will have to cast lots."

A horrified look appeared on Giovanni's face. "Papa, I'm still a child. I can't change the baby's diapers."

Teresa exploded into laughter. "You're just looking for an excuse, Giovanni. If I have to take a turn changing the new baby's diapers, then you have to take a turn, too."

Francesco turned toward Ornella. "What do you think? Should we cast lots to determine who will be on diaper duty?"

Ornella smiled. "It sounds like a good idea to me."

Francesco slapped his thigh. "It's settled then. When the new baby arrives, everyone will serve on diaper duty."

As the children groaned in unison, Francesco turned his full attention toward Ornella. She'd been half-heartedly engaged in the pleasantries. Indeed, the worried look on her face made his stomach clench.

THURSDAY, June 28, 1877

A WEEK LATER, Ornella awoke with a start to the shrill sound of a screaming child. Her heart tensed. She tossed the blankets aside and glanced at the mantel clock. Seventy-forty-five! She had to be at Bible study by nine o'clock.

Francesco's side of the bed was empty. Grabbing her robe from the back of the chair, she wrapped it around her slightly rounding body and hastened to the kitchen to see what was going on. She found Teresa wrapping a bandage around Marco's finger.

"What happened?" Ornella rushed to Marco's side.

Teresa gave her mother a reassuring smile. "Marco cut his finger. It's just a little cut, but it hurts a lot."

Ornella sighed and looked at her son. "From the sound of your screaming, I thought that something terrible had happened."

"Something terrible did happen, Mama." Tears rolled down the little boy's face.

Ornella examined the bleeding finger. "It's only a surface cut, son." She gave Marco a hug. "Finger cuts hurt a lot because of all the nerves in our fingertips."

The child's screaming subsided as he nestled his face into Ornella's robe.

Maternal affection swarmed through her. Why could she not feel this same affection for the child in her womb?

Ornella turned toward Teresa. "I suppose Papa has left."

"Yes, Mama. He left an hour ago. He said he didn't want to wake you since you needed the rest."

Ornella's heart warmed. What a good husband she had! And how poorly she'd treated him! Guilt seeped into every pore of her body.

"Mama, I'm hungry." Marco rubbed his sleepy eyes.

"Nonna will get you breakfast this morning. I need to go to my Bible study."

Just then Nonna shuffled into the kitchen, her soft slippers squeaking on the wooden floor. "So, what's this I hear? A little boy named Marco is hungry?"

Marco giggled. "Yes, Nonna. I'm starving."

She approached him and gently took him by the shoulders. Scanning him mischievously from head to toe, she smiled and raised an eyebrow. "Well, you don't look like a starving child to me." She squeezed his arms. "Look at those muscles." Then she poked his stomach. "And that tummy seems pretty solid to me."

"Aw, Nonna. I'm still really hungry."

Nonna drew Marco into a big bear hug. "So, what would my hungry grandson like for breakfast?"

He looked up at her, eagerness in his eyes. "Sausage and scrambled eggs."

Nonna tweaked his nose. "Ah, sausage and eggs. That sounds like a delicious breakfast to me."

"Will you make it for me, Nonna?"

She lifted his chin and smiled. "How can I say no to a handsome face like yours?"

"You can't!" Marco laughed.

Ornella gave her mother a complicit look. "I see he has you wrapped around his little finger."

Nonna smiled sheepishly. "Of course he does. What do you expect from an Italian nonna? I would not be true to my heritage otherwise."

Ornella chuckled. "Well, let him stay wrapped around your little finger while I go to my Bible study."

With that, she headed back to her bedroom to dress. She didn't want to be late this week. Now that she'd determined to accept the pregnancy and to make the best of it, she needed God's Word and her friends more than ever to keep her afloat.

In a few moments, she dressed and quickly drank a cup of coffee. After gathering her Bible, a notebook, and her knitting supplies, she gave Mama a quick peck on the cheek before heading out the back door. "I'll be back in time for lunch, Mama."

Mama nodded. "God be with you, *figlia mia*."

As Ornella walked into the hot and muggy June day, a deep sense of relief settled over her. She drew in a shallow breath of the humid air that portended another scorching summer day. She should have brought a small flask of water with her. But there was no time to go back to get one.

She proceeded in the direction of the church. Relief flooded her as she checked her pocket watch. This week she would arrive on time.

As she approached the church, yesterday's turmoil lifted. Perhaps it was due to the anticipation of being with women who understood what she was going through. Women who'd been there, albeit in different ways. But women, nonetheless, who understood the complexities of being a woman as men did not. For the next few hours, she would find solace and wisdom in their fellowship. Perhaps she would even recapture some of her former joy.

As soon as she set foot in the church, a blanket of peace settled over her. There was something about being in the presence of God, away from the manifold distractions of daily life, that brought life to her soul. Her heart warming with gratitude, she glanced at the Cross over the altar before hurrying toward the knitting circle meeting room at the back of the church. The Cross that had set her free. The Cross that, as long as she trusted in God, would continue to set her free from every chain that would try to ensnare her.

As she hastened down the hallway, lively chatter filled her ears, indicating that the Bible study had not yet started. She breathed a sigh of relief. Clarissa was a stickler for starting on time—and rightly so.

As she entered the spacious room, the ladies looked up from the table around which they sat. "Ornella! So glad you made it." Miriam's voice rose above the others. After Ornella's earlier episode with nausea, it was clear that Miriam was glad she'd made it, too.

Ebony burst into a grin. "So, do you have any news for us, Ornella?"

Ornella stiffened. She did have news for them. But not good news. At least not in her opinion. She paused and stood in place. "I do have news."

The silence was thick as the ladies leaned forward,

poised on the edge of their chairs, eagerly awaiting her update.

Before replying, Ornella took in a deep breath as she scanned the friendly faces in front of her. Finally, the difficult words burst forth. "I'm pregnant." It was like laying down a heavy burden of guilt that had hung around her neck ever since Ramona had told her she was with child.

To Ornella's great surprise, the ladies broke into loud applause. "Praise the Lord! Hallelujah! Glory to God!" And many other such expressions of joy resounded throughout the room.

Ebony stood up and walked over to give Ornella a bear hug. "Shall I start calling you Aunt Tilly?" Her laughter bubbled throughout the room.

Although Ebony had meant it as a well-intentioned joke, it struck Ornella as the worst of insults. She burst into tears.

Ebony stepped back, a look of alarm on her face. "Oh, Sweetheart, what's the matter? Did I say something wrong?"

Ornella choked out the words. "No, Ebony. No." She hiccupped over a deep sob. "I'm just feeling extra sensitive these days."

The ladies gathered around Ornella, all attempting to comfort her.

But their good intentions only exacerbated her dismay.

Clarissa stepped in. "Let's make room for Ornella to sit down."

As Ornella sat, the sobs came faster and faster.

Clarissa sat down beside her and gently took her hand. "Now, dear one, tell us why you are crying. Why are you so upset?"

Could she reveal to these close friends how she really felt about the baby? That she didn't want this child? That she was angry and afraid about the pregnancy? That she felt trapped? What would they think of her? If they knew the truth, would they still welcome her to their meetings? Would they still look on her the same way? Or would they think she'd fallen away from the faith?

But Ornella could no longer hold it in. The truth begged to be told. If she could not tell these ladies whom she trusted, whom could she tell?

Before she could stop herself, she blurted out the painful words. "I don't want this baby." Then, burying her face in her hands, she sobbed convulsively. "I'm such a terrible person for feeling this way. What kind of mother doesn't want her own child? Will God ever forgive me?"

After a brief moment of hesitation among the women, Ebony was the first to speak. "Ornella, I suppose you be like many other women over the course of history. You think, girl, that every single one of 'em wanted their babies? If so, you're livin' on the moon." She chuckled.

"But one thing makes you stand out from all the rest of them women. You's as honest as the day is long. You admit your true feelin's. Feelin's ain't neither right nor wrong. It's how you act on them feelin's that counts. Ain't nothin' wrong with honesty. When you's honest with youself and with the Lawd, you's on the right track."

Cholena shouted "Amen! Ebony speaks truth."

Ornella lifted her head. Had she heard Ebony correctly? Ornella turned toward her friend. "You mean that my feelings are not wicked?"

Ebony gently placed a hand on Ornella's shoulder. "Wicked? Child, you ain't got a wicked bone in your beautiful Italian body!"

"Ebony's right, Ornella." Clarissa's gentle voice was like warm oil washing over Ornella's shattered soul. "We women experience all kinds of emotions, some positive, some negative. What matters is how we respond to our emotions. What matters is how you will treat your baby. And I know you will be just as wonderful a mother to this new child as you are to your other children."

"Yes, Ornella. Clarissa is absolutely right." Miriam jumped in. "When I got pregnant with my third child, I was depressed for a long time. It wasn't that I hated the baby. It's that I hated how the baby would change my calm and peaceful life. I was tired of constant upheavals, especially since Jacob was always busy at the synagogue. I was also angry because it didn't seem fair that he could go do what he wanted while I had to stay home and handle the children, the house, and everything else."

Miriam's honest admission was like balm to Ornella's soul. Her eyes widened. "That's exactly how I feel. Now that my other children are growing, I'd planned to start pursuing my dream of painting and opening an art gallery here in Cape May."

"That's a wonderful idea!" Cholena clapped her hands in delight. "Don't let something as little as a baby stop you."

The ladies burst into laughter. Cholena was the only single one among them, and, as such, had no children. Good sport that she was, upon realizing what she'd said, she joined heartily in the robust laughter.

Clarissa intervened. "Ornella, we're going to pray for you."

As the ladies surrounded Ornella, Clarissa prayed. "Father God, we thank You for Your love for Ornella. We thank You for this new and precious child You are creating in her womb. You know the emotional struggles Ornella is facing, Lord. And You alone can help her to align her emotions with Your will. Lord, You have given Ornella the gift of art and the desire to paint for Your glory. While we do not understand Your ways, we trust You. You Yourself said in Your Word that Your ways are higher than our ways, and Your thoughts are higher than our thoughts. So, despite this seeming setback in Ornella's pursuit of her artistic dream, we trust that You will use this precious child to further Ornella's dream in a way that she cannot even imagine. In Your Name we pray. Amen."

Everyone shouted "Amen" in response to Clarissa's prayer.

With tears streaming down her face at this outpouring of love from these precious women, Ornella's heart melted. They were her sisters in Christ and would be for all eternity. She was beginning to understand even more deeply the meaning of the Body of Christ and the interconnectedness of all of its members. They needed one another. But the wonderful thing was that they had one another because they had Jesus Christ. They all shared in His eternal life because they were His own. His Body.

Soon afterward, Clarissa began the Bible study, continuing with the topic of trusting God. Ornella listened with rapt attention, taking in every word and making notes along the way of points that particularly ministered to her mind and heart. She would cling to these truths in the days ahead. She would trust God no matter what came her way.

At the close of the Bible study, the ladies shared coffee, tea, and homemade refreshments baked by Miriam and Loretta, and then they bid one another a warm farewell until the following week.

As Ornella made her departure, one by one the ladies of the group offered encouraging words and a promise to continue to pray for her. By the time Ornella left the Bible study that morning, she was emotionally and spiritually refreshed and equipped to face whatever challenge lay ahead. She even began to anticipate the arrival of the new little one within her.

Yet, despite the warm encouragement of her sisters in Christ, a part of her soul still wavered between peace and fear.

CHAPTER

EIGHT

Tuesday, July 31, 1877

AFTER SEVERAL GRUELING weeks of coping with the serious negative effects of the railroad strike among his farmhands, Francesco learned with great relief that the strike had finally ended. United States President Rutherford B. Hayes had ordered federal troops to bring order to the rioting crowds. Since the strikers were not organized, they quickly dissipated, leading to calm once again. At least on the surface. Who knew if the protests would flare up again and when? Francesco would have to keep a close eye on things.

By God's miraculous grace, Mino had survived the gunshot wound, and Tomás had been apprehended and incarcerated. His trial was forthcoming, but from all the evidence, it looked as though he would be convicted.

Finally, thank God, the farm could get back to its normal operations, and Francesco could now turn his full attention to the soon-coming harvest and the preparations for the new baby.

That night at dinner, he warmed at the sight of his family gathered around the kitchen table. "Well, I have some wonderful news. The strike has finally ended."

The children burst into loud cheers.

Nonna laughed while placing both fingers in her ears to drown out the loud noise.

"That's wonderful, Papa!" Teresa's grin was a mile wide.

"Hurray!' Giovanni raised both hands in the air. "Now we can send our crops to Philadelphia again."

Caterina clapped her hands. "And tourists can take vacations again."

Giovanni thrust a triumphant fist in the air. "That means the restaurants will need to buy more of our vegetables."

Ornella agreed. "And that means more income for our family."

Francesco turned toward Ornella and smiled. "God is always faithful to us. He provides all that we need."

Ornella nodded as she patted her rounding abdomen.

Francesco took her hand. "Let's thank the Lord now for putting an end to the strike and for protecting our farm."

As Francesco prayed, deep gratitude filled his heart. In a few short months, one more Lombardi would join them. Who would the child be? A son? A daughter? His heart stirred in anticipation.

But as his gaze rested on Ornella, he worried that her anticipation did not at all match his.

Tuesday, July 31, 1877

That night, as Ornella lay in bed, dread overshadowed her again. Although greatly relieved that the strike had ended, she worried. Would there be aftermaths to the ending of the strike? Would it start up again? Would there be retaliation on the part of those who had lost? Just because the president of the United States had ordered an end to the strike didn't mean there was an end to the opposition against the railroad tycoons.

Even among Francesco's farmhands there were those who vehemently disagreed with the president's orders.

Would those farmhands cause trouble for Francesco and the farm?

Her husband slipped into bed beside her. "You seem concerned, Ornella. Are you not pleased that the strike is over?"

She turned her face toward him. "Of course, I'm pleased. But I still have reservations about the railroad issue. I'm not sure it has been permanently resolved. There are those who disagree with the president's orders and who are still opposed to the railroad's injustices toward its workers."

He took her hand. "Don't worry about what might be, Ornella. Be thankful for what is."

Francesco was right. Why did she have so much trouble living in the now? The now was all she really had. The future was in God's hands. Why could she not simply rest in that truth?

Faith is resting in Me, dear one.

The Lord's words comforted her anxious soul. Yet why did she have so much trouble resting in Him? Why did she find it difficult to trust the One who created her, who knew her better than anyone knew her. No one was more powerful than He. No one more capable. No one more caring. Certainly He could handle the problems of her life far better than she could.

Ornella closed her eyes, remembering the words of the Good Book. *Sufficient for the day are the evils thereof.*

As she reached for Francesco's hand, she determined to take one day at a time and to leave the future in the hands of the only One who knew the beginning from the end.

Yet, would faith prevail over sight as she faced the difficult days ahead?

CHAPTER

NINE

Six Months Later . . .
Friday, December 21, 1877

SUMMER SOON TURNED into fall and fall into winter as Ornella awaited the birth of her fifth child. She'd done her best to prepare as lovingly for this child as she had for her other children. She'd spent the last several weeks sewing several new little garments, including a little coat and cap for the lingering winter days that would lead into spring. She'd also knit two large swaddling blankets and even crocheted a small teddy bear for her new baby.

In a corner of her bedroom, just under the window facing the eastern sky, she'd prepared a lovely sleeping area for her child. With their son Giovanni's help,

Francesco had built a wooden cradle that would be placed in that corner but now stood under the Christmas tree, awaiting the new baby's arrival.

The early morning view from the window in this corner of the room was stunning. Her new little one's soul would be fed watching the sun rise in all its brilliance over the lush farmlands of Cape May. When the weather got warmer, Ornella would open the window and allow the intoxicating fragrance of the honeysuckle tree just beneath the window to float into the bedroom.

With Christmas only a few days away, Ornella busily made the bed and straightened up the bedroom. She found it increasingly difficult to get around and spent a good part of her days resting, waiting for the baby to be born. Despite her efforts to make the best of things, she still struggled with worry and fear. Would this delivery be more difficult than her previous ones because of her age? Would she have the strength to raise the child? Would she love this child as much as she loved her other children?

Although she'd resented her pregnancy in its early stages, with Francesco's and Mama's encouragement, and with the love and prayers of the ladies in her knitting circle, she'd resigned herself to the fact that she was going to have another child and there was nothing she could do about it except to make the best of a difficult situation. As Francesco frequently reminded her, she would try to focus on the good things.

Outside, a light snow fell, blanketing the earth in white splendor. Moving slowly with a heavy sigh, Ornella fluffed the pillows on the large, four-poster bed in which she and Francesco slept. She then straightened the bedspread, smoothing out the wrinkles as best she could.

Yet, as she worked, fear still ate at her. No matter how hard she tried, it would not let go of its fierce grip. It kept her awake at night, causing her to break out in cold sweats. It haunted her in the daylight hours, as she went about her daily chores. It even tried to attack her in those sacred moments of prayer, as she sought refuge in the Lord. Would it ever end?

Just then, Marco rushed into the bedroom, followed by Caterina. "Mama, Christmas is almost here. Can we make *strufoli*? It's my favorite Christmas dessert."

"Mine, too." Caterina clapped her hands. "There's nothing like Christmas honey balls." Caterina's face eagerly awaited Ornella's response.

Ornella placed her hands on her hips. The last thing she wanted to do was to make strufoli. But she couldn't deny her children the fun of making this traditional Italian Christmas dessert. They eagerly looked forward to it each year.

Ornella smiled. "Yes, we can make strufoli. But on one condition."

Marco's eyes rounded. "What's that, Mama?"

"That you promise me that you and your sister won't argue in the process."

Marco and Caterina looked at each other and grinned. In unison they replied, "We promise."

"All right. Let's go down to the kitchen and gather everything we need."

Caterina took the lead. "I'll race you down the stairs to the kitchen, Marco."

Marco took off after her.

Ornella shouted. "No running, children. I don't need any of you hurt, especially right before Christmas."

In a few moments, they had all gathered in the kitchen.

Ornella donned her apron, leaving the strings to hang in front of her because she could no longer tie them around her waist. Soon she would be rid of the extra girth.

"Caterina, please get the flour, sugar, and vanilla extract from the cupboard. Marco, please get two eggs."

While the children collected the ingredients, Ornella retrieved a large wooden bowl in which to mix them and a cast iron skillet in which to fry the honey balls.

The children followed Ornella's instructions and placed the ingredients on the kitchen table. After mixing all the ingredients together, they had great fun rolling the dough into long cylinders and then cutting the cylinders into little pieces which they then rolled into little balls.

Just then Teresa entered the kitchen. "What are you doing?"

"We're making strufoli. Do you want to help?"

Upon Giovanni's soon arrival, all four children participated in the grand venture.

After all the dough had been rolled into little balls, Mama fried the balls in hot olive oil until they were crisp and golden. Afterwards, she placed them on a clean kitchen towel to drain and then onto a large platter. Finally, she dripped warm honey over them.

'Papa will be so surprised when he sees this," Caterina exclaimed.

As the children helped Mama put the last flourishes of decorative candies on the splendid dessert, Francesco walked through the kitchen door.

"Papa! Papa! We made strufoli for Christmas."

Francesco grinned. "I smelled the aroma from one hundred yards away." He winked at Ornella. "Shall we have some now?"

"Yes, please, Mama! Let's have some now and then again on Christmas Day."

Ornella smiled. "Yes, you may all have some now. Teresa, please put out some bowls and spoons for everyone. I'll make some coffee."

For the next hour, the family enjoyed the delicious fruit of their labor. As they finished eating, Giovanni announced, "When I grow up, I'm going to teach my wife how to make strufoli."

"Why don't you make them yourself," Caterina asked, "instead of making your wife do all the work?"

Ornella intervened. "Caterina has a good point,

Giovanni. Perhaps you can make strufoli together with your wife, just as you did with us today."

"I know what I'll do. I'll make it for my wife so she won't have to do any of the work."

"Now that's a good thought, Giovanni." Papa smiled and then planted a kiss on Ornella's cheek. "I need to repair that broken cupboard shelf you've been complaining about."

Ornella gave him a slanted look. "Complaining? Better to say the shelf I've asked you to fix a hundred times."

"That's what I said. Complaining." He walked away laughing.

After putting the remaining strufoli in safekeeping for their upcoming traditional, seven-fish Christmas Eve dinner, Ornella returned to the bedroom to finish straightening up. Strange sensations coursed through her swollen body. Would the baby come soon?

FRIDAY, December 21, 1877

AS SHE REACHED HER BEDROOM, a sharp twinge sliced the side of Ornella's abdomen, flooding her soul with panic. She doubled over in pain. Was it time? Ramona had estimated her due date to be in late

December, around Christmas. Only four days remained until that special feast.

She glanced out the bedroom window. The snowfall had grown heavier, and thick white clouds hung low over the horizon. What if Ramona couldn't make it to deliver the baby? What if there were a complication? What if she died during childbirth?

Ornella's muscles tensed as another contraction shook her body. Were they still too far apart to send Francesco to fetch Ramona? She prayed a silent prayer that nothing would impede the midwife's delivering the baby and that she herself would survive.

Giovanni entered the bedroom, interrupting her thoughts. "Mama, will the baby be here in time for Christmas?"

She reached for her older son and took his hand. "I think so, but I'm not sure. Babies have a way of coming when they're ready to come."

Giovanni frowned. "But Papa and I made the baby a Christmas gift. I want him to get it in time for Christmas."

Ornella managed a smile. "You still think you're going to have a little brother, don't you?"

He nodded. "I hope so. Caterina wants a sister, but we have enough girls in the family."

"Enough girls? We have the same number of each: two boys and two girls."

"That's what I mean. If we get another girl, then we'll have more girls than boys."

Ornella chuckled. "And what's wrong with that?"

"If we get another girl, then Marco and I will be outnumbered."

"And is that a bad thing?"

"When it comes to being outnumbered by girls, it is."

"How so? Please tell me."

"Well, girls are sneakier then boys. They keep secrets, and we boys never know what they're up to. That means they can trick us better."

Ornella held her side. "Oh. Do you mean that girls can outwit boys?"

"Yes. And boys don't like it one bit."

Ornella stifled a smile. "I see."

Just then, Caterina ran into the room. "So there you are, Giovanni. I've been looking all over for you."

Giovanni quirked an eyebrow. "Why?"

"You were supposed to help me clean the kitchen after breakfast, and you left."

Giovanni lifted his palms toward Ornella. "See what I mean?"

"Giovanni, go help your sister clean up the kitchen right now. You know that is your chore for this week. Why did you try to shirk it?"

Giovanni pouted. "I hate cleaning the kitchen."

Ornella drew in a breath. "What if I told you that I hate cooking your breakfast?"

A surprised look crossed Giovanni's face. "You do? I thought you loved cooking."

"I do, but I don't like to cook for people who are ungrateful and won't do their part in helping the family."

Giovanni glared at his sister. "All right. You win, Caterina."

A moan escaped Ornella's lips as another contraction struck her.

"Mama, what's wrong?" Caterina was at her side.

"I think the baby may be coming."

Still another contraction shot through her, this one more forceful. "Caterina, call your papa. I think it's time."

Caterina's eyes grew wide. "Yes, Mama! Right away!" She ran out of the room and headed for the kitchen, shouting, "Papa! Papa! Come quickly! Mama is about to have the baby!"

Within a couple of minutes, Francesco stood at Ornella's side. "Is it time?" Although he'd been through Ornella's labor four times before, his face still showed concern.

Ornella nodded, perspiration dotting her forehead. "Yes. Go fetch Ramona." She squeezed his hand. "Quickly, Francesco!"

"Yes. Right away." He motioned toward Caterina. "Caterina, stay here with Mama, and help her get into bed. I will be back in a few moments."

Caterina gave him a wide-eyed look. "Okay. But hurry, Papa! I'm scared."

"There's nothing to be afraid of. Just do what I say. I will be back soon." With that, he ran out of the room.

About twenty minutes later, after what seemed to Ornella like an eternity, Francesco returned with Ramona. She rushed into the bedroom where Ornella lay on the bed, moaning softly.

Relief flooded Ornella's soul. "Thank God, you're here."

Ramona took off her coat and laid it on a chair near the bed. In an instant, she was at Ornella's side. "How frequent are the contractions?"

"About every two minutes."

Ramona smiled. "We're getting close then. Now just relax as best you can. Take deep breaths. You've been through this before, so you know what to expect."

Ornella nodded and then released a long, low moan.

Tensing, Francesco sat on the other side of the bed, next to Ornella. He took her hand in his and squeezed it gently. "The Lord is with us, dear one. All will be well." He prayed under his breath.

Ornella squeezed Francesco's hand. "The pains are getting stronger."

Ramona wiped the beads of perspiration from Ornella's forehead. "We're getting closer. This child should come fast."

"Oh, I hope so!" Ornella squeezed her eyes shut at

the next onslaught of excruciating pain.

Ramona placed a tightly rolled up piece of cloth between Ornella's teeth. "Bite on this when the pain gets severe. Meanwhile, I will check for the position of the baby."

As Ramona examined her, Ornella glanced at Francesco. His eyes reflected the concern of her own heart.

She tightened her hold on his hand as the contractions grew stronger. Although she'd given birth four times before, this time something was different.

She bit down hard on the tightly rolled-up cloth the midwife had placed between her teeth to help ease the unbearable pain. But it did no good. The pain only worsened, searing her body like hot iron on flesh. She let loose a blood-curdling scream.

"Try to stay calm, dear one," Ramona said.

But the midwife's words brought no comfort.

Another scream burst from Ornella's lungs. "God, have mercy!" One more agonizing contraction, and she would surely die.

The midwife sat at the foot of the bed, gently massaging Ornella's abdomen. "Soon it will be over. A bit more patience."

But Ornella had no more patience. She wanted this baby out, and out now! "Please! Can you do something? Anything?"

The midwife shook her head. "I've done all I can

humanly do. The rest is up to God."

A new contraction rocked Ornella's weary body like a high-magnitude earthquake, shaking her to the core of her being. Would she die from the pain? Or from the delivery?

"Relax, Ornella." The midwife spoke in gentle tones. "I see the head crowning. Soon you will hold your baby in your arms."

That moment couldn't come soon enough.

Searing pain rocked Ornella's lower body as another wave of contractions struck her. She shrieked in agony as her body took over and forced the baby to be born.

Suddenly an infant's cry pierced the air.

"A girl!" The midwife shouted. But then, a gasp, and nothing more. Only a look of horror on her face as she hesitated to give the child to her mother.

"What is it?" Ornella shrank back upon seeing Ramona's face and shouted. "Ramona, tell me what's wrong?"

Slowly, the woman turned the baby toward Ornella.

A primal, guttural scream more excruciating than the physical pain of childbirth rose from the depths of Ornella's soul and escaped her lips. She averted her gaze. "O God, no!" She slammed her fisted hands on the bed sheet and fiercely shook her head. "No! No! No!"

Ornella ventured her gaze again toward Ramona. The mid-wife's blood-stained hands held a Mongoloid child.

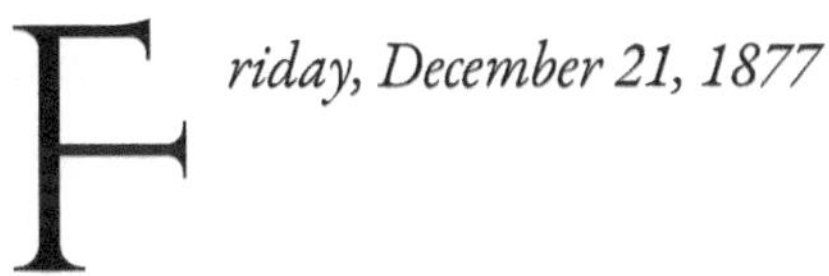

riday, December 21, 1877

FRANCESCO'S BLOOD curdled at the sound of Ornella's agonizing scream. It was more than the scream of childbirth. It was the scream of hopelessness. Of piercing anguish. Of primal despair.

At the sight of his new child, Francesco's mind froze in suspension between disbelief and reality. Was he having a nightmare? Was he only imagining that his child had been born abnormal? Or was it true?

As he stared at the infant, he could not deny the evidence on the baby's face. A face at once beautiful and freakish. Attractive and repulsive. Endearing and offensive, cutting the very heart out of him. He turned his head away, unable to grasp the painful truth. What had he done to merit this tragedy? Where had he sinned? What was wrong with him that he had produced a Mongoloid child? Surely, a curse rested upon him.

Drowning in tormenting guilt and shame, he dared to turn his gaze again toward the infant. Fear and worry overpowered him. What kind of life would she have? How would she cope? Would she be accepted by society, or shunned in horror?

Hot tears stung his eyes as he stifled a sob. Unable to move, Francesco wiped his face with the palm of his hand. A lump lodged in his throat. This was his child. His own flesh and blood. It was his God-given duty and responsibility to care for her. To protect her. To provide for her. Compassion flooded his heart. He would move heaven and earth to care for this innocent one, no matter how difficult it was to look upon her disfigured face.

Blinking back stinging tears, he swallowed the lump in his throat. At all costs, he must hide his horror from Ornella. His guilt. His remorse. His shame. He must be strong for her. And for his other children.

Ornella turned her gaze toward him, her eyes two wells of infinite pain.

His gaze locked on to hers in the mutual silence of shock, denial, and despair.

"Francesco." Ornella's words were barely a whisper.

"Francesco!" She wailed and broke down into wrenching sobs as she reached for him.

Brushing back her dampened hair, he leaned toward her and cradled her head in his chest. No words came. Only gut-wrenching tears of anguish that streamed down his face. He held her for a long moment.

Still in Ramona's arms, the baby screamed.

Her ear-piercing cry unraveled the strings of Francesco's heart. "Ornella, the child needs to eat. You are the only one who can feed her." His words were an attempt at encouragement. An attempt to rekindle her purpose in life. An attempt to keep her soul from dying.

She turned her head away. "I can't." Her voice was hoarse. "I can't bear to look at her."

"But, Ornella, you must. The child will starve if you don't feed her."

Ramona stood by Ornella, her voice pleading for the baby in her arms. "Ornella, she needs you."

Maternal instinct tugged faintly at Ornella's heart. Reluctantly, she took the child from Ramona's extended hands and placed the babe against her breast, forcing herself to look upon her.

As one starving, the infant eagerly began to suckle and kept her innocent gaze fixed fast on Ornella's eyes.

Francesco tensed at the sight of this first mother-child encounter. It could set the tone for their entire, lifelong relationship. He prayed a silent prayer that God would turn Ornella's pain into power, and her ashes into beauty.

Ramona interrupted his thoughts. "I must fill out the birth certificate. What do you wish to name her?"

Despite several conversations prior to the baby's birth, he and Ornella had not decided upon a name. He turned toward Ornella. "What name would you give her?"

Ornella spoke without hesitation. "Mara, meaning *bitter*. For she has brought bitterness to my life."

At her words, the cracks widened in Francesco's already broken heart.

~

FRIDAY, December 21, 1877

AFTER RAMONA LEFT, numbness overtook Ornella as the aftershocks of the sudden emotional earthquake continued to rock her. Violent winds of fear buffeted her mind as she pondered what lay ahead.

Visions of spending the rest of her life caring for an abnormal child bombarded her, inciting a burning sensation in the pit of her stomach. How would she do it? How would she take care of a baby who required so much special attention? Attention Ornella had no strength left to give. For surely, Mara would never be able to care for herself if she lived beyond the few short years that Mongoloid children usually survived.

Ornella's throat ached from incessant sobbing. Would her suffering ever end?

And what of her own dreams and aspirations? Would she have to give them up yet again? And this time forever?

Physically and emotionally drained, she leaned her head against the pillow while Mara suckled fiercely. Ornella cringed at the sight of the baby's abnormal face. Her imperfect face. The slanted eyes. The flat nose. The short neck. The face of a child born out of keeping with Ornella's plan. But as much as Ornella tried to avert her eyes, her gaze instinctively kept returning to her baby.

Why did she feel only repulsion for her child?

At the sight of Mara's clear, innocent brown eyes, a spark of tenderness welled up in Ornella's heart. Perhaps if she tried hard enough, she could actually love this child. Oh, how she wanted to! Her baby deserved her love just as much as her other children did.

A sliver of compassion penetrated Ornella's heart. Mara had not asked to be born this way. She hadn't asked to be born at all. None of this was her doing. The child was not to blame. If anyone were to blame, it was Ornella and Francesco. Physical intimacy in marriage often resulted in children.

Mara's gaze was locked intently on Ornella's. She had

Ornella's dark eyes. Yet her gaze reflected a transcendent joy that Ornella had not observed in her other children.

A faint stirring took hold of Ornella's heart.

Mara grabbed Ornella's thumb, her grip tightening with what seemed like a fierce and desperate cry for love. Steeped in grief, Ornella struggled to push through the insurmountable barrier that stood between them.

She turned toward Francesco, seated at her side and patiently watching and waiting. "I suppose we should call in the children."

Francesco nodded. "Yes. I'm sure they're eagerly waiting to meet their new sister."

Ornella looked up at him, foreboding circling her rib cage. "But you must prepare them first."

Pain lined his face. "Yes, I agree." While Francesco went to prepare and fetch the children, Ornella looked at the infant in her arms. "Lord, give me some feeling for this child other than repulsion. Please, I beg you. I am numb with grief. I do not know how I can go on."

Mara stared at Ornella, a desire for connection in her newborn eyes. Eyes that spoke what her lips could not.

A tear rolled down Ornella's cheek. Her baby needed her. No matter what her feelings, and no matter what the cost, Ornella would not fail her. But did caring for her child mean failing herself?

Just then Francesco entered the bedroom, followed by the children. They came quietly. Tentatively. Their eyes wide with questions. No one spoke a word.

Marco was the first to approach the bed to meet his new baby sister. His eyes widened. "Mama, she's beautiful!" Wonder laced his voice. "May I touch her hand?"

Mara's gaze turned toward him, filled with delight at the presence of a new little person.

"Yes, my son. But be gentle. She is only a newborn baby."

Marco reached for Mara's other hand. When she gripped it, he broke into a broad grin. "Mama, Mama! She's squeezing my hand!"

Marco made no mention of Mara's appearance. If he noticed it at all, he looked beyond it. Why could Ornella not do the same? Why did she not feel the same tenderness? The same compassion? What kind of monstrous human being was she to feel repulsion toward her own flesh and blood?

Guilt for her unnatural feelings washed over her. Was she sad because she longed for what might have been instead of what was? Sad because her heretofore perfect life had now become imperfect? Sad because being the mother of an imperfect child made her imperfect? Was this God's punishment for something she'd done?

She managed a smile for Marco's sake. "Yes, my son. Your little sister loves you."

Marco grinned. "And I love her, too."

His response pried open a trickle of warmth in Ornella's heart.

By now, the other children had gathered around the bed. "May I hold her, Mama?" Teresa's smile was as wide as the Adriatic Sea along which Ornella had grown up.

"May I, too?" Caterina was next to make her plea.

Giovanni was the only one who held back.

Francesco placed a hand on his older son's shoulder. "Would you like to hold her as well, Giovanni?"

He looked up at his father. "I'm afraid I'll drop her." Giovanni turned his gaze toward Mara. "But when she's old enough, I'll do some of her chores for her."

Papa chuckled. "You must love Mara a lot if you are willing to do chores for her."

Caterina gave him a quick retort. "Yes, Giovanni. You probably love her more than you love me."

Giovanni scowled. "Well, Mara doesn't talk back to me the way you do."

Caterina put a hand on her hips. "Well, of course not! She hasn't learned how to talk yet, silly. But just wait till she does."

Uneasiness stirred in Ornella like dark clouds announcing a storm. Would Mara ever learn to speak properly? Would she do the things that normal children did?

Francesco gathered his brood. "Now, children, Mama and Mara need their rest. Let's give them some time to recover, shall we? You can all spend more time with Mara later."

Marco reluctantly let go of Mara's little hand and followed his siblings as they filed out of the bedroom.

Ornella turned to Francesco. "I wish I could be as happy as they are about the new baby."

Francesco took her hand. "In time, dear one, you will be."

Ornella leaned her head against the pillow. But could she ever be happy about a child she could not even bear to look at?

CHAPTER
ELEVEN

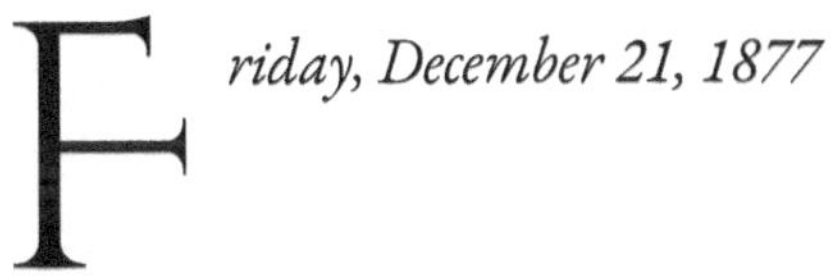

riday, December 21, 1877

AFTER THE CHILDREN LEFT, Francesco asked himself the same question. Given enough time, could he ever be as happy about the new baby as the children were? Truth be told, he wasn't sure.

Not only had Mara's birth altered his entire life, but it had also caused the family dynamics to shift in some profound way. Things were different. He sensed it. At least between him and Ornella.

And he was afraid.

She seemed distant. Lost in her own world of pain. Enveloped by a thick cloud of suffering he could not penetrate. How could he reach her to comfort her? What would happen to their marriage if she did not come out of this? To their family?

Dread snaked over him, threatening to coil itself around his soul.

His muscles tensed as he gazed out the bedroom window. In the distance, the setting sun reminded him that the children needed dinner. Ornella was in no condition to do much of anything, exhausted as she was from having given birth only a short while before and broken-hearted at having delivered a Mongoloid child. An imperfect child, she'd called her.

Francesco struggled to school his thoughts as anguish gripped his heart. He rose from the bed and checked on the infant now lying sound asleep in her crib. Strands of thin black hair edged the crown of her little round head. Tiny hands lay fisted on either side of her cherubic face. Were it not for her slanted eyes and flat nose, she would be a perfectly beautiful baby. But her facial features screamed that she was not normal.

A dark sense of foreboding circled Francesco's rib cage and squeezed the heart out of him. What kind of life would Mara have? What obstacles would she face that his other children would not face? How could he raise her in such a way as to survive the unique challenges that surely lay ahead?

Fear threatened to consume him. If he weren't careful, he could fall into despair. But he would not allow himself to do so. He would trust in the God Who was able to get him through anything that life cast his way.

Francesco turned his attention toward Ornella, now asleep in the bed. A cascade of dark, tangled curls, highlighted by strands of gray, framed her pale face. Wrenching sobs, which now had melted into the merciful rest of sleep, had left tear stains on her dampened cheeks. Would that sleep alone could forever remove her pain! His heart ached for her. Oh, how he loved her!

After covering Ornella with another blanket, Francesco made his way toward the kitchen below. The children were gathered around the table eating homemade chicken soup while Nonna sat with them, overseeing their antics.

"Papa!" Marco exclaimed. "Where are Mama and Mara?"

Francesco took his seat at the head of the table. "They are both sleeping. They've had a hard day."

Nonna offered him a bowl of soup, but he refused. "Thank you, Mama, but I don't have much of an appetite."

The old woman looked concerned. "But you must eat something, Francesco. You need your strength."

His mother-in-law was right. "Very well. Give me just a little please."

She ladled a scoopful of hot soup into a small bowl and served it to him.

Its aromatic blend of chicken and spices stimulated his palate. He thanked her and took a mouthful. As he swallowed, the warm broth brought comfort to his cold and shattered heart.

Mama took a seat next to him. "The Lord will bring good out of this situation, Francesco."

He agreed. "I know so. But meanwhile, it is a very difficult situation to face."

The old woman nodded. "While Ornella is recuperating, you must be strong for the family. This has been an enormous blow to her."

How well Francesco knew. "I will do my best. Please pray for all of us."

"I have been, and I will continue to pray." She patted his hand and then rose to get the children more soup.

Despite her sometimes irritating, old womanish ways, Ornella's mother was a prayer warrior. And the family certainly needed prayer.

Giovanni interrupted Francesco's thoughts. "Papa, why are Mara's eyes slanted?"

Francesco's breath hitched. Now that the questions had begun, he must prepare to answer them. He paused for the right words. "Your baby sister was born with an abnormality, Giovanni."

"What's an abnormality, Papa?"

Francesco chose his words carefully. "It's something that is not normal."

Marco held his spoon in mid-air. "Mara seems normal to me. What's not normal about her?"

"Her body is different from a normal body." He suppressed the tension rising at his children's incessant, yet innocent, questioning.

Caterina quirked an eyebrow. "How is it different, Papa?"

"Well, to name a few differences, her eyes are slanted, her nose is flat, and her neck is short."

Marco slurped his soup. "So what's wrong with that?"

Marco's innocence touched Francesco's heart. "That's a good question, Marco. I suppose on the surface there's nothing wrong with that. But those external features are a sign of some possible medical problems that Mara may have as she grows older."

Ever the practical one, Giovanni offered his perspective. "But who doesn't have some kind of problem, Papa?"

"This is true, my son. Life is full of problems."

Marco glared at Caterina. "You're right about that, Papa. My biggest problem is sitting right over there." He pointed to his sister.

Caterina stuck her tongue out at him.

"Now, children. Please. Let's be kind to one another. This is a very difficult time for Mama. She will need a lot of kindness from all of us."

A quiet thoughtfulness settled over the children.

"And now, are there any more questions before we clean up the dinner dishes?"

Caterina sat straight up in her chair. "I have one, Papa. What makes a body normal?"

"I suppose it is a body that looks like most other bodies. With normally formed eyes, nose, arms, and legs."

Marco protested. "But I don't look like Caterina. Does that make me abnormal?"

"No, it just makes you different."

Caterina jumped in. "I always knew you were different, Marco."

Marco scowled at his sister and then answered Papa. "So maybe Mara is normal but just different. Like all of us."

Oh, to have the perspective of a child! Unlike adults, they could see to the core of an issue. They could separate the wheat from the chaff. Francesco did not need to worry about explaining such matters to his children in a way they would understand. Unlike adults, they were the ones who truly understood.

Giovanni's intense gaze caught Francesco's eye. "But why is Mara abnormal, Papa?"

"Only God knows, my son. But your sister is a precious human being, just like all of us. We will love her and bless her in whatever way we can."

"Papa, why doesn't Mama like Mara?"

Teresa's perceptive words sliced Francesco's soul. Had all the children noticed the truth as well?

His eldest daughter's question unnerved him. Yet, she deserved a response. "Your mama is in a state of shock. She expected Mara to be born a normal child. This sudden and surprise turn-of-events has shaken Mama." He sighed. "But she will be all right. We must all help her through this. We are family, and we help one another, especially during tough times."

Giovanni turned to Papa. "I'll take out the trash every day, Papa, and I'll even help wash the dishes."

Caterina clapped her hands. "It's a miracle!" She turned toward Papa. "See, Papa. Mara is already causing good things to happen in our family."

A lump formed in Francesco's throat. Yes, God would turn this seemingly bad situation into something of great good. That was His promise.

Now if only Ornella would believe it.

~

FRIDAY, December 21, 1877

JUST BEFORE MIDNIGHT, Mara's shrill cry awakened Ornella from a deep sleep. Half-dazed, she rose, grabbed her robe from the chair, and hurried to the crib. Her body ached, but her heart ached even more. For a short time, sleep had drowned reality in the sea of forgetfulness. But now, wakefulness slammed truth against her consciousness like the sudden aftershock of an earthquake.

A moonbeam shone through the curtains, illuminating the baby's face, now red from screaming. Ornella gently lifted her from the crib and tried to soothe her with words of comfort. But Mara kept screaming. It was all Ornella could do to keep from screaming herself. The child would not be comforted. How could Ornella go on like this, day after day? She would go out of her mind.

Where was God in all of this? Did He not see her agony? Had He played some sort of cruel joke on her, suddenly changing the course of her well-planned life and plunging her into the pit of despair?

A tremor shook her body. No sooner had she thought the dishonoring thought than heat rose to her face. "Forgive me, Lord. I don't know what's come over me. Please help me!"

After changing Mara's diaper, Ornella settled into the rocking chair to feed her. The gentle, back-and-forth motion of the chair instantly quieted the infant. She began to suckle, all the while gazing intently at Ornella as though searching her very soul. The pure innocence of the child's eyes stirred guilt in Ornella's heart.

Why did she have such negative feelings toward her

own baby? Why did the child who should elicit compassion draw forth repulsion instead?

Ornella studied her baby's tear-stained face. White flecks dotted the dark irises of Mara's eyes, while small, low-set, folded ears rested on either side of her small head.

The little palm Mara curled tightly around Ornella's finger displayed a single crease across the middle, while the large gap between her first and second toes only reminded Ornella yet again that she had borne an imperfect child.

Imperfect. Why did the word trouble her so much? Was there such a thing as a perfect child? A perfect human being? A perfect anything on this earth?

Of course not. Yet imperfection implied inferior, did it not? Short of perfect.

As she nursed Mara, Ornella's mind drifted back to her fifth birthday, shortly before her father abandoned her. Mama had planned a party and invited Ornella's little friends from the neighborhood.

Celebration was in the air as all the children came, dressed in their Sunday best and bearing delightful gifts for the birthday girl. As the children immersed themselves in the festivities, Ornella blew out the candles on her cake. While Mama cut the cake, Ornella's father unexpectedly burst into the room in a drunken stupor.

"What's going on here? What's all this trash on the

walls of my house?" Enraged, he tore the decorations off the walls, thrusting them to the floor in a crumpled heap.

Ornella froze in panic as shame bore into her soul. Time stood still, imprisoning her in a wall of rejection.

While Mama vainly attempted to pacify him, Papa approached Ornella, a scowl on his slovenly face. "Whose idea was it to give you a birthday party? Don't you know you don't deserve one. Look at you, an imperfect, good-for-nothing. You can't do anything right. You never measure up. You're a disgrace to the family name." He spat at her. "I wish I'd had a son." From his eyes, fiery darts of hatred flew toward her. "Even more, I wish you'd never been born."

Ornella's heart crashed into her rib cage, splintering into a million pieces. Her world collapsed around her. Papa hated her and didn't want her because she didn't measure up to his standards. Would she ever be good enough to earn his love? Would she always fall short? If she wanted Papa's love, she must strive to be perfect. Nothing short of perfection would please him. Nothing short of perfection would win his love.

After Papa's tirade, the guests left quickly, not wishing to incite further embarrassment for Ornella and her mother. Ornella spent the rest of the afternoon sobbing in Mama's arms. No matter how much Mama tried to comfort her, the damage had already been done.

And the damage still lingered, permanently etched on Ornella's soul like letters carved on stone.

She leaned her head against the back of the rocking chair and sighed. Ever since that life-shattering incident, she'd hated imperfection. Imperfection meant not good enough. Unacceptable. Imperfection meant falling short of the standard required for acceptance and love.

She swallowed the painful lump that rose to her throat. Imperfection had meant the loss of her father's love. His rejection. His scorn. If she wanted love and acceptance, if she wanted to have worth, she had to be perfect. Perfection meant measuring up to her father's standards. Only then would he accept her and love her.

So, she'd striven to be perfect. She'd planned her life so that it would be the perfect life. The kind of life that would win the acceptance and love of others. The kind of life she, and no one else, must control to ensure that it remained perfect. She would allow no one else to take control.

But life in the person of Mara had rammed into her walls of perfection. Mara had knocked down those meticulously built walls. And life would never be the same.

Ornella's gaze drifted to Francesco, sound asleep in bed. Life would never be the same for him, either. As much as he'd valiantly tried to hide his shock, it had not escaped her. She winced at the memory of his face upon seeing the baby for the first time. The memory of shock mingled with grief, of horror wrestling with compassion motivated by his tender heart.

She blinked the mist from her eyes. What would this tragedy do to him? To their marriage? To their family?

Ornella gazed at the child now sleeping in her arms. The infant had no idea of the power she'd wielded in Ornella's life. Of the havoc she'd wreaked. Of the anguish she'd caused.

Yet it wasn't Mara's fault. But, if not her fault, whose fault was it?

Tears drained down the back of Ornella's throat. Why did she torment herself with such questions? Questions that would never be answered, at least not this side of Heaven. In the long run, did it matter whose fault it was? Did it matter that her world had been turned upside down? No. What mattered was how she responded to what happened.

But that was the problem. She didn't know how to respond. She'd entered new territory. Unfamiliar territory, with new challenges, new expectations, and new rules. She didn't know how to navigate this new world of abnormality. This new world where she no longer had any control over her life.

This new world had new rules. Unfamiliar rules. Rules she did not like, but rules she had to abide by in order to survive. The *status quo* of former days had drastically altered, leaving her in a world she'd never known existed.

She fought despair as she cried out to her Maker. "O

God, I'm dying inside. Rescue me from this pit! You are my only hope."

A cord wrapped itself around Ornella's stomach and tightened.

Trust in the Lord with all your heart and lean not to your own understanding. Clarissa's teaching at the last Bible study surfaced to Ornella's mind. Truth be told, she wasn't trusting in the Lord at all, let alone trusting Him with all her heart. Instead, she was leaning to her own understanding. Her own reasoning. Her own way.

A shiver coursed through her. Isn't that what she really wanted? Her own way? Her own plans? Her own perfect life?

But didn't she have a right to a life of her own? A life that fulfilled her own needs? Must she always sacrifice her needs for the needs of others?

She had to get a hold of her life. To regain control before it was too late. But how?

TWELVE

S aturday, December 22, 1877

SUNLIGHT STREAMED through the window when Ornella awakened the next morning. Francesco's side of the bed was empty. He must have left early for town with William to purchase farm supplies.

Disappointment surged through Ornella at Francesco's absence. She'd hoped to see him before he left. To talk with him for a few moments about Mara. So many concerns filled her heart. So many things they needed to discuss. He'd seemed quite preoccupied because of the child. Although he would never admit it, Mara's physical deformity had struck him hard.

Ornella blinked back salty tears and rose to check on the baby. After awakening several times during the night, Mara had slept soundly until early morning, affording Ornella some much needed rest. Now the infant lay wide-awake, her bright eyes mesmerized by the sunlight forming dancing patches across the inner lining of the crib, like so many musical notes tapping out a happy tune.

Ornella paused, the baby's wonder eliciting her own. Despite her physical abnormalities, Mara's mind seemed normal. She was acutely observant of her surroundings and extra sensitive to the slightest changes in Ornella's mood. Ornella would need to be more careful in relating to her.

She lifted the baby from the crib, checked her diaper, and then ventured forth from the bedroom. Mara's limp body dangled weakly in her arms, requiring more support than a normal child. She worried that more physical challenges lay ahead.

She found Mama in the kitchen, busily cooking breakfast and feeding the children. Ornella smiled. "Good morning, children."

"Mama!" Marco jumped from his chair and ran toward her. After giving Ornella a quick hug, he focused his attention on Mara. "Good morning, little sister." He reached for her hand.

Mama was at Ornella's side, sorrow and fatigue lining her eyes. '*Buon giorno, figlia mia*. It's good to see you up.

Would you like some breakfast?"

"Good morning, Mama." Ornella nodded. "Yes. I need to eat something. I haven't eaten much since yesterday. I need to keep up my milk supply."

Mama pulled out a chair for her. "Here. Sit down. I will bring you some eggs and sausage."

Marco stood by Mama's chair. "Is Mara going to have breakfast with us?"

Ornella managed a smile. "No. Mara cannot eat solid food yet. She will be nursing for several months."

Marco looked at Mama. "Did I drink only milk when I was a baby?"

"For the first few months, yes. But then you began to eat regular food."

Mama placed Ornella's breakfast on the table in front of her and took the baby from her arms. "Eat, *figlia mia*. You need your strength."

While the children bombarded her with questions, Ornella stole small bites of her breakfast. It was good to be with them again. Their positive attitude toward their new baby sister encouraged her, removing a bit of the darkness from her life.

"So, what have my children been doing while I have been tending to Mara?"

Caterina chimed up. "Taking out the trash."

Ornella raised an eyebrow.

Giovanni put down his fork. "And washing the

dishes." His eyes gleamed. "Aren't you proud of us, Mama?"

Ornella's heart warmed. "Of course, I'm proud of you. And I am thankful for your help." She turned toward Mama. "What time did Francesco leave?"

"About an hour ago. He said that he and William wanted to get an early start on their trip to town for supplies."

"Mama, now that Mara is here, we can have an extra special Christmas celebration." Giovanni's rounded dark eyes filled with hope. "This will be her first Christmas."

Christmas. Ornella had not given it a second thought. How could she celebrate Christmas when her heart was broken? She wanted to cancel Christmas this year.

But she couldn't disappoint her children. She had to get a grip on herself. She could not turn back the clock. Mara's abnormalities had happened, and the sooner Ornella faced that truth, the better. Not only for herself but also for her family.

She would burn the bridges behind her. She would not turn back. Did not the Scriptures command her to forget those things that were behind and to press forward? She drew in a deep breath. Yes, she would press forward. In truth, it was her only choice. The alternative would mean destruction and despair.

"When Papa gets home, we'll make plans for Christmas Day."

The children shouted for joy, startling Mara. She began to cry.

Marco's eyes widened. "What's the matter with Mara, Mama? Doesn't she like Christmas?"

"She's never experienced Christmas. But I think she was startled by the sudden shouting. You will have to keep your voices down until she gets used to our boisterous family."

A disappointed look crossed Marco's face. "I'm sorry. I'm just excited about Christmas."

"I know, son. But we will have to learn to make some adjustments for Mara." *Many adjustments.*

"Okay, Mama." Marco let go of Mara's hand and walked away, dejected.

Christmas would arrive in three days, and there was much to be done. The seven-fish Christmas Eve meal needed to be planned and prepared. Gifts had to be wrapped, and outfits chosen for the children to wear to church. Ornella would need Francesco's help. She would talk with him when he returned from work.

The children finished eating. "How can we help you today, Mama?"

"Perhaps you can clean your rooms and make sure your homework is done."

Giovanni made sure to clarify. "We don't have any homework, Mama. We're on Christmas vacation."

"Very well, then, you can read a good book. I need to talk with Nonna for a few moments." Ornella motioned for Mama to sit down in a chair next to her. "And don't bicker," Ornella warned as the children left.

Mama sat down and turned toward Ornella. "How are you feeling today?"

"Still in a daze, Mama. Still grieving." She sighed. "But I've decided to stop looking back and to move forward instead."

"That is wise, Ornella. Looking back to try to recapture the past never did anyone any good. The Good Book commands us to look forward."

"And that's what I want to do. But the problem is that I don't know the next step to take to move forward. This situation is foreign to me. I've never had a deformed child before. I've never had the worries I have now with her. How to best take care of her and to make sure she is cared for as long as she lives." She pushed down the sob in her throat. "How to give up my art career yet again." A twinge of anger poked at her heart. "My whole world is different now, Mama. And I don't know which way to turn."

Mama nodded. "The Lord will help you, Ornella. And I am here for you as well. I will help you in whatever way I can and as much as I can."

"Thank you, Mama." Ornella paused. "What troubles me most is that I no longer have control over my life. I am at the mercy of circumstances. And I don't like that feeling. Up until Mara came along, I had my whole life planned. And everything was going according to my plan. I even spoke with a gentleman in downtown Cape May about renting his storefront for my art gallery." A tear trickled down her cheek and dropped onto Mara's chest. "Now I have to tell him that I cannot rent his space after all."

"Ornella, don't be so quick to give up your dream."

Ire rose within her. "But, Mama. Let's be practical. How can I be a professional artist and run an art gallery while raising a child who requires much more attention and care than a normal child?"

"It won't be easy, but, with God's help, you can do it."

Ornella shifted in her chair, her heart heavy. "Mama, I'm not sure God wants me to be an artist."

"Why do you say that? Surely He would not have given you artistic talent only to bury it under a bushel."

"Well, then, explain to me why He gave me a defective child?" The bitterness in her own voice took Ornella by surprise.

"I don't know why certain things happen, Ornella. But one thing I do know. Nothing bad comes from God. Mara's birth is not a punishment. And He did not allow her to be born for the purpose of keeping you from your art." Mama's gaze locked onto hers. "Perhaps this child is a catalyst for your art."

A catalyst for your art. Mama's words triggered a spark of hope in Ornella's soul.

Ornella sighed. "Well, for whatever reason, I no

longer have control over my life. And I don't like that one bit."

"Ornella, when we follow Christ, we surrender the control of our lives to Him. Perhaps that is what you need to do. Scripture tells us that man makes his plans, but God orders his steps."

Upon hearing that verse, Ornella stiffened. Was that her problem? Rebellion? Had she only *thought* she'd surrendered her life to Christ but had not truly done so? But what of her dream? Had God not given it to her? If so, why did she have to surrender that to Him as well? God did not take back His gifts.

"I'm not even going to try to understand it all, Mama. I'm simply going to do what I can to get through each day."

But in every fiber of her being, she doubted she'd make it.

Saturday, December 22, 1877

It was eight o'clock by the time Francesco left with William for the supply store in downtown Cape May. Although planting season was still three months away, Francesco wanted to be sure he had what he needed in case of another railroad strike or some other unforeseen calamity. The strike earlier that year had taught him how dependent he was on the railroad for his livelihood. He must find a way to become more self-reliant.

Loosely holding the reins, Francesco guided the two old mares as they plodded along the gravelly dirt road leading to town. In unison, their hoofs clip-clopped in a steady rhythm that echoed in the crisp, morning air. From the nearby ocean, a light breeze, bearing the smell of sea salt, brushed against his face, prickling his skin. Ahead of him, several wagons loaded with hay traveled to neighboring farms with a supply of winter food for the horses.

The day was cold and cloudy, resembling the climate of Francesco's heart. The birth of Mara had sent Ornella into a downward spiral of despair, one from which she seemed unable to extricate herself. Despite his many efforts to comfort and encourage her, she seemed lost in her world of sorrow.

Francesco sighed. The grayish-white color of the sky signaled an imminent snowfall. Despite Cape May's proximity to the ocean, winters could be brutal. He hoped that the snowstorm would hold up until evening.

Francesco's mind drifted to Ornella. He'd left her fast asleep after she'd spent a long night of tending to Mara. The child had awakened several times during the night to eat and to be changed. Ornella was exhausted. Although he'd helped her with the diaper-changing, he could not help her with the feeding. So, while Mara still slept, he did not awaken Ornella, although he'd wanted so much to embrace his beloved wife before he left.

The sorrowful look on her face even as she lay asleep still haunted him. In all of their married life, never had she been so despondent.

The rickety old wagon rumbled loudly, past pedestrians carrying knapsacks headed for a day of work in town or some last-minute Christmas shopping. To the side of the road, finches darted in and out of the tall reeds in a lively game of hide-and-seek.

"So, how be the new little one, and how the missus be?" William's rich, bass voice interrupted Francesco's thoughts.

Word had quickly gotten out to the farmhands the day before that Ornella had birthed a Mongoloid child. At some point, Francesco would have to face his men's questions, but he wasn't exactly sure yet how to do so. But William's question came from one who was not only an employee; he was also a friend and a brother in Christ. William would understand and maybe offer him some wise advice.

"The baby seems to be doing fine, William. But Ornella is having a hard time of it. A very hard time. Seems as though she's not the same woman I married." He sighed. "I'm worried about her and don't know what to do to reach her."

William shook his head. "It's gotta be hard for the both of you. The shock of it all and then the concern of raising the child. For sure Miz Lombardi's heart be broken. Ain't no mamma want her child not to be perfect."

"But I don't understand why her heart seems closed to the child. She doesn't have the maternal instinct for this child that she has with our four other children."

William turned toward him. "That be tellin' you the depth of the shock. It went real deep and hit somethin' on the inside of her that the Lawd wanted to touch."

"What do you mean?"

"The touch of the Lawd is always a healin' touch. Miz Lombardi must be needin' healin' of somethin' on the inside that's keepin' her from livin' in the full freedom Jesus died to give her."

William's words were like a stroke of lightning suddenly illuminating the darkness. "I suppose I need that healing touch, too, William. Mara's birth was a big shock to me as well. I'm still reeling from it." Francesco drew in a deep breath. "But I don't feel repulsed by Mara as Ornella does. I feel compassion for the child."

"Been my 'sperience that the good Lawd always be diggin' deep into our hearts to remove what don't belong there. And He do that by allowin' trials in our lives. Sometimes real tough ones." William paused. "Like me, for instance. The Lawd had to dig real deep into my heart to show me that the fear of man be keepin' me from receivin' the abundant life He done died to give me." William sighed. "And he showed me by allowin' me to lose my job 'cause I was compromisin' and tryin' to please my friends instead of pleasin' the Lawd." William shook his head. "That kind of livin' ain't never gonna work."

Francesco's curiosity was roused. "What happened after you lost your job?"

"I went through a tough time of not havin' work. My wife and kids went hungry fer a spell. But when I repented before the Lawd, he done turned that awful situation into somethin' good." William turned toward Francesco. "He led me to work for you." His straight, white teeth flashed a broad smile. "And I ain't never had a better boss than you."

Francesco's heart warmed. "Why, thank you, William. And I can honestly say that I've never had an employee as honest and as faithful as you."

"Thank you, sir. Like the Good Book say, the good Lawd done turned them ashes into beauty."

Francesco nodded. "If it weren't for the Lord, I don't know what I'd do."

William leaned forward, his palms between his knees. "Time was years ago when my granpappy and granmammy had a little boy born blind. At first, they was beside theirselves with grief. But turned out that that boy done became a preacher and won thousands of souls to Jesus."

Francesco widened his eyes and glanced at William. "Is that right?"

"Yes, sir. Reminds me of that Bible verse that promises that all things work together for good for those who love the Lawd."

Francesco grew pensive. How was God going to work everything out for good for him and Ornella? The way things looked now, he couldn't see anything good coming out of the situation with Mara except more heartache for Ornella —and for himself as well.

CHAPTER

THIRTEEN

T *uesday, December 25, 1877*

C HRISTMAS MORNING FOUND Ornella dragging herself out of bed before dawn. She'd been up at least four times the night before to feed Mara and had no strength left to face the festivities of Christmas Day.

Nor the heart.

The night before, with Mama's and Teresa's help, she'd made her best effort to prepare and celebrate their traditional, Italian seven-fish dinner, and, after the children had gone to bed, she and Francesco had wrapped gifts for them. Today, they would have a simple meal before the children opened their gifts.

While Mara was still asleep, Ornella quickly dressed and headed downstairs to the kitchen to make coffee. As the coffee percolated, she looked out the window. A heavy snow had fallen during the night, blanketing the ground in crystals of white. Perfect for sledding and building a snowman. The children would be delighted.

And their outdoor play would give her time to rest.

She poured herself a cup of coffee and went into the parlor. Her Bible, now covered with a layer of dust, lay on the table where she always kept it. She hadn't read it much since she'd learned of her pregnancy, so distraught had she been with the news. Then, after Mara was born, Ornella hadn't read it at all.

Lovingly convicted by the Holy Spirit, she settled into the sofa and opened the pages of the well-worn book. The book that had been her mainstay for so many years. Her gaze landed on Psalm 147: 3: "He healeth the broken in heart, and bindeth up their wounds." The comforting words jumped out at her. Mara's birth had broken her heart. But right there in His Word, God said that He healed broken hearts. No wound was beyond the scope of His ability to repair it.

A tear trickled down Ornella's cheek. She needed God's help. She needed to know the why of her negative feelings toward Mara. Then she needed God's help to get rid of those negative feelings.

Marco burst into the room. "Mama! Mama! It's Christmas Day!"

He settled into the sofa beside her and nestled his head on her chest. "I can't wait to open my presents."

Ornella tousled his dark, curly hair. "What makes you think you got presents?" she teased.

Marco lifted his head. "I always get presents on Christmas Day."

"And what would you do if I told you there are no presents for you this year?"

His eyes widened. Then he laughed. "I wouldn't believe you!"

Ornella tapped his nose with her finger. "And you would be right!"

It was so easy to love Marco and the rest of her children. Why was it not easy to love Mara in the same way?

Giovanni burst into the room. "Merry Christmas, Mama! Did you see the snow?"

"Yes." He sat down next to Marco. "Hey, Marco. Do you want to go sledding with me?"

"Sure! Let's go." Marco started to rise.

Ornella placed a hand on his shoulder to restrain him. "It's only six o'clock in the morning, Marco. Let's have Christmas dinner first and then you can spend the afternoon playing in the snow."

Marco groaned in disappointment.

At that moment, Caterina entered the room. "Can I go sledding with you, too?"

"Only if you help me take out the trash."

Caterina frowned. "Okay. I will."

"Mama." Marco turned toward Ornella. "When will Mara be able to go sledding with us?"

Ornella's stomach muscles tightened. "Probably not for a few years." Would Mara ever be able to go sledding?

Giovanni frowned. "A few years? That's a long time, Mama. I can't wait to teach her how to sled."

Teresa appeared at the entrance to the parlor. "Good morning, everyone. Merry Christmas!" She settled into a chair across from Ornella and yawned. "How can I help you today, Mama?"

Teresa's gentle heart warmed Ornella's own. "You can help me prepare the noonday meal."

Teresa smiled. "Of course, Mama."

"And I will help you, too." At Nonna's cheerful voice, Ornella smiled.

"Good morning, Mama."

"Merry Christmas, Nonna!" The children shouted in unison."

"*Buon Natale*! Merry Christmas!" Nonna smiled and took a chair across from Ornella. "I see that all of my grandchildren are awake extra early today." Her eyes twinkled. "I wonder why."

Marco raised both arms into the air. "Because it's Christmas, Nonna, and we get presents, that's why!"

Just then, Papa entered the room. "What's all the ruckus? You would think it's Christmas or something."

The children burst into laughter.

Giovanni stood. "Papa, you're so silly. It *is* Christmas!"

Francesco chuckled. "Well, what do you know?"

Just then, Mara's cry pierced the air.

Her heart sinking, Ornella sighed and rose from her chair. For a moment, she'd been lost in the former world of her perfect family. But now, reality had struck her once again. Her family was no longer perfect. A new member had been added. An imperfect member. And with that new member, the family's former equilibrium had shifted. The family was now out of balance. No longer perfect. Wobbling.

Would it finally topple?

~

Tuesday, December 25, 1877

That night, after the children had gone to bed, Francesco sat in their bedroom, watching Ornella rock Mara to sleep. The day had gone reasonably well. With Mama's help, Teresa had prepared a good meal for the family. Afterward, the children had opened gifts as little Mara watched intently.

When Giovanni brought Mara the new cradle he had made for her with Papa's help, she'd gurgled in delight, giving the impression to the children that she understood exactly what was going on. After the exchange of gifts, the children spent the afternoon sledding. It took a lot to convince Marco that Mara was too young to join them.

Francesco studied his wife. Throughout the day, she'd been distant and detached. Not her usual joyful self. She'd gone through the motions of living but lacked her usual spark of life within.

Francesco tensed. "Did you enjoy the day, Ornella?"

She lifted her gaze toward him. "Do you want the truth?"

"Of course I want the truth. I've never known you to speak other than the truth."

"I had a miserable day, Francesco."

"I'm sorry, Ornella. Do you know why?"

"Of course I know why." She rose and placed a sleeping Mara in her crib. As she headed back toward the rocking chair, Francesco stood and took her into his arms.

To his dismay, her body stiffened beneath his touch. She withdrew from his embrace.

"Ornella, what's the matter? You seem so distant since Mara's birth."

She averted his question.

"Ornella, what is happening to you? To us?"

She shook her head. "I don't know, Francesco. I have lost all will to live."

"But why? This is so unlike you."

She fisted her hands. "Why? You ask why? Are you

blind? Do you not see that we have produced an imperfect daughter? A Mongoloid?"

He squared his jaw. "Of course I see the physical imperfections. But why do they bother you so much? Why do they prevent you from loving our child? Can you not focus on the ways she is perfect?"

"Perfect? Are you insane? There is nothing perfect about her, Francesco. She is a monster." Sudden remorse etched her face.

Francesco dragged trembling fingers through his hair. "Ornella! You must stop this. Your attitude is affecting our marriage. Our children. Most of all, it is harming you."

She burst into tears. "I don't know how to stop it, Francesco. I wish Mara had never been born. She has destroyed every hope I had of following my dream."

He was at his wits' end. "Why don't you talk with Clarissa. Maybe she can knock some sense into you. Apparently, I can't."

"Some sense into me?" She rammed into him. "If *you* had any sense, you'd understand how I feel. You're not even trying to understand."

"Ornella, I've done everything I know how to understand you. I suppose at this rate, I never will."

With that, he rose and left the room, leaving behind a sobbing wife.

CHAPTER

FOURTEEN

*T*wo *months later*
Monday, February 25, 1878

TWO MONTHS HAD TRANSPIRED since Mara's birth, yet Ornella's despondency had not diminished but had only grown worse. Francesco was at a loss as to what to do. A wall had arisen between then, blocking out virtually any form of deep connection other than superficial conversations.

And even those had become strained.

A part of Ornella had died, and with it, a part of their marriage had died as well.

A deep and dark chasm lay between them, one Francesco doubted he could ever bridge. Ornella had pulled away not only from him and their newborn child, but also from their other children, and from life itself. What could he do to call her back? Could he call her back?

He sat on the edge of their bed, his folded hands hanging between his knees. His heart heavy, he struggled to find a way to comfort his wife. No amount of encouragement helped her. Instead, it only made things worse.

He gazed at Ornella, sitting across from him in her rocking chair by the window. Night had fallen as they prepared to retire.

His heart overflowed with love for her. "Ornella, what can I do to comfort you?" He lifted both hands in a pleading gesture. "I am at a loss."

"There is nothing you can do." She lowered her eyes. "I feel trapped."

The word startled him. "What do you mean *trapped*?"

"This child has put me in a prison. I can no longer even think of painting, let alone of opening an art gallery. My freedom has been stolen."

"You are not thinking straight, Ornella."

"What do you mean I'm not thinking straight." Daggers edged her voice.

"You are not thinking straight in blaming the child. Mara is innocent. How can you blame her for your situation and your feelings?"

She turned on him, fire in her eyes. "Who else is there to blame? Were it not for the child, I wouldn't be in this situation nor have these feelings."

Francesco forced himself to remain calm. "If you have to blame someone, blame me, not the child." Francesco shook his head, releasing a long breath of frustration. His heart racing, he rose from the bed and paced the room. What was going on? What was happening to his wife? To their marriage? She'd become a stranger to him. Had she lost her mind? Was she sick? He had to do something, but what? "You are making no sense, Ornella."

Ornella turned on him. "Oh, so I'm making no sense? Is that what you think? I'll show you what making sense is. Making sense is treating women with the same equality with which one treats men. It's allowing them to pursue their dreams just as men are allowed to pursue theirs. It's not keeping women at home, cooking, cleaning, caring for children their entire lives if they don't want to stay there."

"But how am I not treating you with equality? And who is forcing you to cook and clean and care for our children? Is this not what we agreed upon when we married? You would take care of the home and I would work to support the family?" He raked his calloused fingers through his graying hair.

Kneeling before her, he took her hands in his. "Ornella, God made men and women equal in value but different in function. We were designed to do different things. We have different roles to play, but this doesn't mean that one gender is inferior to the other. That one gender is of less value than the other. Nor does it mean that you cannot paint and open an art gallery if you want to."

She jerked her hands out of his grasp. "But you're not a woman. You have no idea how I feel."

He blew out an agitated breath. "I'm trying to understand how you feel." He wiped a hand across his face. "It wasn't my idea to make woman the gender to bear children." His patience seeping out of his pores, he stood and waved a dismissive hand in the air. "If you have a complaint, please discuss it with God, not with me. I have no answers for you."

The temperature between them had grown hot. Francesco had to do something to keep it from rising even more, especially since the Bible forbade their going to bed angry.

He turned toward her yet again. "Ornella, having another child doesn't mean you can't still open an art gallery."

Her eyes flamed. "What do you know? You work in the fields all day while I take care of the children. How would you like to have to take care of a baby while working in the fields? You could never do it. And neither can I run an art gallery while taking care of an infant." Her face flushed with anger.

"But you can bring the baby with you."

"Of course." Sarcasm dripped from her words. "Just as you could bring the baby to the fields."

His patience was on its last leg. "An open field is far different from a sheltered art gallery."

"So how am I supposed to do that? You try talking with customers while tending to a crying baby."

"But the baby won't always be crying. Nor will there be customers every single moment. Surely there will be a few moments to tend to them when they come."

Her mouth twitched as she shouted in his face. "You are nothing but a blockhead."

Her words shook his equilibrium. In all their years of marriage, never had she spoken to him in such an unkind manner. Something was seriously wrong. "Dear one, you are making something big out of nothing."

She turned on him. "How dare you say that! You've never been in my shoes. You have no idea what I'm going through."

Never had he witnessed such bitterness in her demeanor. Surely there was more going on in her heart than met the eye. Perhaps she was seriously ill. In the past, Ornella had looked forward to every other pregnancy. Of course, it had been their mutual desire to have four children, so that desire had played into her attitude. But this pregnancy was unplanned. Unexpected. And, sad to say for Ornella, unwanted. Francesco's heart grieved for their newborn daughter.

He tried again to appeal to Ornella's reason. "Perhaps we can hire someone to take care of the baby while you are at the gallery."

"And with what money? I would have to make a profit first before I could hire anyone to help me."

He reached for her but she withdrew. "Don't touch me! You don't understand what I'm feeling, and you never will."

Francesco's heart sank. What was happening to his wife? Should he call the doctor? He didn't recognize her anymore.

He stood and drew her from the chair, pulling her into his arms.

This time she yielded. Cradling her head in his shoulder, she broke into violent sobs.

The rapid palpitations of his heart threatened to burst through his chest.

"Ornella, what is happening to you? To us?"

But in her anguish, she remained silent.

MONDAY, February 25, 1878

A FEW HOURS LATER, at the sound of Mara's strident cry, Ornella rose, wrapped her long flannel robe around herself, and glanced at the mantel clock. It was approaching midnight and the third time Mara had awakened her.

Exasperated at yet another interruption, Ornella checked on the child. She had just finished eating only moments before. A diaper check showed no need for a change. Yet Mara continued to cry.

Ornella reached for the infant and lifted her from her crib. Her face was red from sobbing. Anguish flooded Ornella's soul at the sight of the tear-filled, slanted eyes that gazed back at her. Every time she looked at them, a sword pierced her heart. Would she ever grow accustomed to them? Would they ever incite love and not repulsion? Would she ever be able to accept this child whom God had given her? Did she even want to?

This last thought frightened her to the core. Had she not frequently promised the Lord that her life belonged to Him, to do with as He saw fit? Yet now, that promise seemed like an empty shell. Meaningless. Lacking truth and sincerity.

Her nerves already frazzled, Ornella carried Mara to the rocking chair and sat down. The child instantly grew quiet. She seemed to know that soon the soothing, rocking motion would begin.

The only thing that comforted her was the back-and-forth motion of the rocking chair. Yet, Ornella could not spend the rest of her life rocking a baby.

When Ornella offered her milk, Mara refused to suckle. Ornella checked her diaper again. It was dry and clean. Why had the child awakened her? What did she want?

Irritation flooded Ornella's soul. "Why did you wake me if you're not hungry or wet?"

At Ornella's words, Mara burst into a loud wail.

Guilt-ridden at her angry outburst, Ornella drew the infant close to her chest and began to sing an old Italian lullaby that she used to sing to her other children. At the memory, tears of nostalgia pushed through from behind her lids and warmth began to fill her heart. She'd enjoyed those earlier days singing to her other babies. Why couldn't she enjoy singing to Mara? What was different now? Mara was no less a human being than her other children.

But she was an abnormal human being.

At the sound of the lullaby, Mara's wailing instantly stopped and a deep peace settled over her.

Ornella studied her round face, her soft skin, her thin, flimsy hair. A sudden wave of compassion flooded her soul. How could she be so callous toward a helpless child, especially an abnormal helpless child? Where had this callousness come from?

All she needs is love, dear one.

The Lord's words pierced Ornella's heart.

Mara fixed her gaze on Ornella. Despite the slanted eyelids, her eyes were intelligent eyes. They reflected an understanding that went beyond the natural and into the supernatural. There was something special about this baby. Something ethereal even.

A shudder coursed through Ornella's body. She suddenly sensed a strong spiritual presence hovering over Mara, as though she were directly connected to the heart of God from whom she'd come. It was as though the aura of heaven had followed her into the earth.

Through clear, innocent eyes, Mara smiled at her, a smile that chipped a tiny piece off the hard shell that had formed around Ornella's hurting heart, opening a tiny wedge in it. A drop of compassion filtered through that wedge.

Ornella's eyes misted. Mara was but a helpless baby, totally dependent on her for her sustenance and survival. She could not take care of herself. Unless someone cared for Mara, she would die.

And so it is with you, dear one. Unless you depend on Me, you will die.

Heat rose to Ornella's face as shame convicted her. Yes, like every child—like every human—Mara needed love. Not just the love that provided for food, clothing, and shelter. No. Like every human being who'd ever lived —no matter his physical or mental condition— Mara needed a deeper kind of love. A love that fed the soul. For there existed a hunger greater than physical hunger. It was the hunger of the soul for human touch, human companionship and relationship. No outward circumstance of health, nor wealth, nor education could eradicate this inner need for love. It was universal.

Mara needed this kind of love. Perhaps even more than most because she was born with several strikes against her.

But could Ornella give her that kind of love? Could she overcome her repulsion toward the child's deformities? Could she look beyond her own selfishness to feel her baby's pain? Surely infants were people. Little people. They might be smaller in size, but they had feelings just like grown people.

Ornella sighed. She'd failed her child by withholding her love. But was she really withholding it when she felt no love in her heart to give?

"O God!" Ornella whispered a desperate plea for help. "Give me Your love for my child, for I have none of my own to give."

CHAPTER
FIFTEEN

T *hursday, March 14, 1878*

A KNOCK on Ornella's door one lovely afternoon toward the end of winter caught her by surprise. She hadn't been expecting anyone and was in no mood for a visit.

Wiping her wet hands on her apron, she quickly hurried to the front door and opened it. She gasped. There before her stood all five ladies of her Bible study group.

"Surprise!" A brilliant smile on her face, Ebony's loud voice pierced the brisk, late winter air.

Ornella drew in a deep breath. "Why, this is certainly a surprise! Please come in."

Despite her emotional and physical unpreparedness, her heart warmed at seeing her friends once again.

After hugs all around, she led them into the parlor and urged all of them to make themselves at home. "Let me call my Teresa. She will prepare some hot tea and apple cake." To her relief, Ornella had just baked an apple cake that was still warm.

Ornella called for Teresa who had been baking with her in the nearby kitchen.

Teresa promptly responded. "Yes, Mama?" Upon seeing all the ladies seated in the parlor, she broke into a big smile. "Hello, everyone."

"Hello, Teresa," the ladies responded in unison. "My, you've grown into a beautiful young woman."

Teresa blushed. "What can I do to help you, Mama?"

"Would you please make some hot tea for the ladies and bring in the apple cake?"

"Yes, Mama. Right away." With that, Teresa left to prepare the refreshments.

Clarissa spoke next. "We had to take advantage of this beautiful day and come visit you." She gave Ornella a big smile. "Frankly, we've been concerned about you."

Ornella stiffened, afraid to lay bare her heart to these precious women. "That's very kind of you."

"Yes, Ornella." Loretta jumped in. "Since you haven't

been to Bible study in several weeks, we were worried. Are you all right?"

Just then, Teresa returned with the tea and cake.

Relief flooded Ornella's heart. While Teresa distributed the refreshments, Ornella would have time to collect her thoughts—and to shield her heart.

When Teresa left the room, Miriam's gaze caught Ornella's. "We've been praying for you, Ornella. Is there anything more we can do to help you?"

"Thank you for the prayers, Miriam. Prayer is what I need most. With the four children and my mother, I've had all the practical help I need for day-to-day activities."

A pause ensued. "Well, where is the little one? May we see her?"

Ornella cringed at Cholena's questions. Although Ornella was touched by her friends' visit, she had not visited them first for the very fear of having them see her Mongoloid child. But now that her sisters in Christ were here in front of her, she could not deny their request without seeming rude. "Yes, of course. I'll go get her."

Ornella excused herself for a brief moment and, her heart pounding, soon returned with Mara in her arms. Ornella handed the baby to Cholena first.

As Cholena took the child in her arms, her eyes widened as an almost imperceptible shadow crossed her face and flickered before disappearing. "Ornella, she is precious."

Mara squealed and kicked her little legs as Cholena uttered words of greeting to her.

One by one, each of the ladies took a turn at holding Mara. By the time the child had made the rounds, she was ready for a nap. Ornella returned her to her crib and then rejoined the ladies.

"So, what has been happening with all of you?" Her feeble attempt to engage in conversation hung heavy in the air.

"We came here to check on you, Ornella." Clarissa's gentle voice pre-empted the others. "When you stopped coming to Bible study, we assumed you needed some support. Know that we've been praying for you."

Ornella's heart softened. What a treasure these women were! Her dear sisters in Christ. 'Yes, it's been very difficult for me. And for my family. As you can well imagine, Mara's condition came as quite a shock. I am still recovering from it."

"Well, don't hesitate to call on us for help.' Loretta's eyes reflected deep compassion. "We are here for you."

"And don't miss any more Bible studies." Ebony's joyful laughter filled the parlor. "It's not the same without you."

After a special time of fellowship, the ladies left, leaving Ornella caught between compassion and condemnation.

* * * *

Saturday, April 6, 1878

WHILE THE VISIT from her Bible study group three weeks before had blessed Ornella and warmed her heart, it had also emphasized how shame at birthing a Mongoloid child had kept her away from the very support she needed.

This morning, she awakened with a strong sense that she should pay a visit to Clarissa. Perhaps her wise friend could help her out of the pit of despair that had gripped her since Mara's birth.

After asking Mama to take care of the children, Ornella packed a bag of supplies for Mara, placed her in her baby carriage, and set out on the half-mile trek to town toward Clarissa's home.

The day was crisp and clear, edged with the first signs of spring. Alongside the road, purple crocuses peeked under brown winter shrubbery while a robin twittered happily in a nearby budding maple tree. White, cumulus clouds, carried on the backs of a brisk ocean breeze, sailed across a pale blue sky. Ornella breathed in the fresh air. After a cold, harsh winter, it was refreshing to be outdoors again.

As she pushed Mara's carriage, she savored the sight of tall reeds bending to her left and to her right. Along the path, vendors pulled wooden carts laden with fresh produce and homemade goods for sale in Cape May. Ahead of her, a horse-driven wagon carried fishermen to their work at the docks.

As Ornella entered the town center, she passed the storefront she'd hoped to rent for her art gallery. Her heart sank at the memory of her forsaken dream. The space had been turned into a needle arts store that would probably remain there for years to come. She stifled the bitterness that rose to her throat.

Upon reaching Clarissa's home, Ornella tensed. Had she done the right thing in coming? What would Clarissa say after Ornella's long absence from Bible study? For the past several months, she'd floundered on the cliff of despair, slipping dangerously toward its edge. She desperately needed someone to put a rope around her and pull her back to sanity and safety.

She pushed aside her anxious thoughts and turned onto the sidewalk in front of Clarissa's house. On either side of the sidewalk, at the head of two small patches of green grass, stood a cluster of pink and purple tulips that bobbed their delicate heads in the gentle breeze. To the side of the house, a large lilac bush was regaled in lavender blossoms that emitted a fragrance sent from heaven. Everything about Clarissa's home spoke peace.

Ornella parked the carriage on the front sidewalk and

withdrew a sleeping Mara from under her mound of soft blankets. With her baby swaddled cozily against her chest, Ornella climbed the three steps to the spacious, wrap-around porch and knocked on the front door.

Within seconds, Clarissa appeared, a broad smile on her face. "What a blessing to see you, Ornella! Please come in."

Heat rose to Ornella's face. She was thankful that Clarissa did not press her for a reason for her absence from yet another Bible study even after their encouraging visit.

The older woman glanced at the child in Ornella's arms and grinned from ear to ear. "Your precious new baby! May I hold her once again?"

Still embarrassed, Ornella reluctantly handed Mara to Clarissa.

With twinkling eyes and a tender smile, Clarissa cooed softly to the child.

Mara cooed in return, the gleeful sound of her little voice emanating sheer delight in the human exchange.

Ornella's chest tightened. Clarissa treated the child as though nothing was wrong with her. Why couldn't she do the same?

Clarissa motioned to Ornella to follow her. "Come, let's sit in the parlor. Make yourself comfortable while I go get us some tea and cake. Then we can chat."

Ornella followed Clarissa and Mara into a cozy parlor filled with sunlight flooding it from two tall, arched windows that overlooked a lovely garden. Clarissa returned Mara to Ornella while she went to fetch the tea and cake.

As Mara fidgeted in her arms, Ornella took a seat on the blue, floral-patterned sofa and laid the child beside her, placing a large throw pillow in front of her to protect her from rolling off.

The sweet scent of lavender and honeysuckle drifted through the open window. Fresh lilacs nestled happily in a white porcelain vase on a small table in front of the sofa. On the fireplace mantel, an old gilded clock softly ticked the relentless passage of time.

Ornella studied the beautiful surroundings. The room was decorated in soft shades of pale blue and white—a calming palette, much like Clarissa's personality.

On the wall hung a painting of Christ the Good Shepherd watching over His sheep as they grazed peacefully in a lovely, sun-filled green meadow. Ornella sighed. How she longed for that kind of peace once again!

Clarissa returned with the tea and cake and settled in a chair next to Ornella. Her gaze shifted to Mara. "She has grown even more beautiful since I last saw her, Ornella."

Ornella's stomach clenched. "How can you say so?" The words spilled out of her mouth before she could stop them. Fire rushed to her cheeks.

Clarissa looked at her in surprise. "Dear one, how can you *not* say so?"

Guilt washed over Ornella, threatening to drown her. Why had she come? Instead of comfort, Clarissa had condemned her and only confirmed that she was an awful mother. An awful woman. An awful person. "But she's a Mongoloid, Clarissa! How can she be beautiful?" Ornella burst into tears. All the pent-up grief of the last several months burst forth like a dam giving way.

"What is it, Ornella?" Alarm edged Clarissa's voice. She rose and placed an arm around Ornella's shoulders.

For a few awkward moments, Ornella sobbed uncontrollably. Then, lifting her head, she looked at her dear friend. "I'm sorry, Clarissa. I didn't mean to cast a pall over our visit."

Clarissa shook her head. "There is no need to apologize, Ornella. Now tell me. What is going on inside you? What lies are you believing?"

"Lies?" What a strange question! Ornella had never considered she might be believing lies.

Clarissa nodded. "Yes. Lies. Tormenting emotions stem from lies. There is a lie—or more than one—that you are believing that is causing your suffering. To be set free, you must identify the lie, renounce it, and then replace it with the truth. We must ask the Holy Spirit to reveal the lie and to show you the truth. Only the truth sets us free from lies and gives us peace."

Ornella worked her lower lip. "But how can I identify the lies?"

"That is the work of the Holy Spirit. He promises to lead us into all truth. If, that is, we want to know the truth." Clarissa smiled. "And I know you do."

"Oh, I do want to know the truth, Clarissa. Where do I begin to identify the lies?"

"First we begin with prayer. We ask God to show you the truth in your situation. To show you the real reason you feel the way you do about your child. So, let's do that now, shall we?"

Clarissa prayed a fervent prayer that the Holy Spirit would expose the lies causing Ornella such pain and that He would reveal the truth that would free her from those lies.

Ornella responded with a heartfelt "Amen!"

Clarissa patted her on the hand. "Now, the next thing you need to do is to consider what you are thinking."

Ornella raised an eyebrow. "What I'm thinking?"

"Yes, every feeling has a thought behind it. Whether the feeling is positive or negative, it has a thought behind it. And the thought behind every feeling is either true or false."

Ornella struggled to grasp what Clarissa said. "Are you saying that feelings are either true or false?"

"No. I'm saying that feelings are what they are— positive or negative. The thoughts behind the feelings are either true or false. While some feelings are backed by truth, most feelings are backed by lies. So we cannot always trust our feelings to speak truth to us. Our feelings often lie to us."

"But how can I know when my feelings are lying to me?"

"When the thought behind the feeling contradicts what God says about that thought in His Word, then the feeling is lying to you."

Ornella shook her head. "I'm sorry, Clarissa, but I'm having trouble understanding what you're saying. Can you give me an example?"

Clarissa tapped her chin. "Let's take your feelings toward Mara. A mother's God-given natural instinct is to love her child. When she does not, then that mother is believing a lie either about herself or about her child. So, with God's help, you need to identify the lie you are believing. First of all, you need to discern whether the lie is about you or about Mara."

Ornella lowered her eyes and searched her heart. "I often think that Mara is inferior to my other children because she is abnormal."

"What do you mean by abnormal?"

"She is not normal physically like my other children."

"What is abnormal about her?"

Ornella fisted her hands. "I think it's obvious. Look at her facial features. Her slanted eyes. Her flat nose. Her thick neck. These are not normal for a human being."

"So, you think that Mara is imperfect?" Clarissa's gaze burned away the dross.

Ornella's face grew warm. "Yes." Her voice was a hoarse whisper. "Yes, that's what I think."

"Well, what does imperfect mean to you?"

Ornella wanted to get up and run away. "I don't know, Clarissa. All I know is that the fact that Mara is a Mongoloid greatly distresses me."

"Are we not all imperfect in some way, dear Ornella?"

"I suppose so. But Mara's imperfection is different."

"In what way?"

"I expected to bear a normal, healthy child. Like the rest of my children. Mara is not like them."

Clarissa gently prodded. "So your expectation of bearing a normal child was not met, correct?"

"Yes, exactly."

"And that makes you angry?"

Ornella's stomach quivered as she struggled to speak the truth. "Yes, it does."

"Why does it make you angry?"

Weary with the continuous barrage of Clarissa's questions, Ornella couldn't handle this grueling conversation much longer. "Clarissa, before I learned I was pregnant, I had planned to resume my painting and to open an art gallery. Mara's birth crushed my dream." She lowered her eyes. "And, I suppose I'm angry about that."

Clarissa placed her hand on Ornella's. "So, at the end

of the day, you did not get what you wanted. You did not get the life you planned."

Ornella bristled. How could Clarissa understand? She'd never had an abnormal child. She'd never had a dream beyond being a homemaker and raising a family." Are you implying that in wanting to pursue my dream, I wanted my own way?"

Clarissa paused. "I see two issues here, Ornella. The first is the shock you've experienced from Mara's abnormality, and the other is the anger you bear toward her for interfering with your pursuit of your dream."

Clarissa's words spoke directly to Ornella's heart. She nodded.

"But is it true that Mara's birth and her abnormality must stand in the way of your dream?"

"How can they not? How can I pursue my dream when I have to take care of her for the rest of her life?"

Clarissa's eyes reflected compassion. "I sense that you are having trouble accepting Mara."

Guilt washed over Ornella. "Yes. I am."

"So we need to discover what lie you are believing that is keeping you from accepting your child as she is." Clarissa furrowed her brows. "Let me ask you, Ornella, what thoughts do you think about Mara?"

Ornella shifted uneasily on what felt like God's witness stand. "I often think that she is imperfect. All I see when I look at her are her imperfections."

Clarissa continued to probe. "So I ask you again, Ornella, what does *imperfect* mean to you?"

Ornella bit her lip. When would the interrogation end? "It means not perfect."

"And what does not perfect mean to you?"

Just then, Mara awakened with a cry.

Ornella leaned over and picked her up.

Mara quieted down as Ornella drew her close to her shoulder. "I think we need to go, Clarissa. It's almost noon, and I left Mama alone with all the children."

Clarissa rose. "I'm so glad you came." She hesitated. "Have you considered doing some sketches of Mara?"

"Sketches of Mara?" The thought seemed unthinkable.

"Yes." Clarissa gave her an encouraging smile. "And perhaps you could eventually turn them into a painting —or a series of paintings."

Clarissa's suggestion intrigued Ornella in a strange sort of way. "I will consider it." She embraced her friend and left quickly, more distressed than when she'd arrived.

TUESDAY, *April 23, 1878*

LATE THAT NIGHT, after everyone had fallen asleep, Ornella sat alone in the parlor, her Bible open on her lap to the Book of Jeremiah. Her gaze fell to Jeremiah 17: 9: "The heart is deceitful above all things, and desperately wicked: who can know it?"

She sighed. Had Clarissa been right in her observations? Had Ornella's heart deceived her and kept her from seeing the truth about herself? About Mara? How could she know?

She couldn't. Only the Holy Spirit could show her what was in her heart. She bowed her head in prayer. "Holy Spirit, show me what is in my heart. I want to please You in everything I think, say, and do. But I need Your help."

Ornella mentally reviewed her conversation with Clarissa earlier that day. The dear woman had spoken of identifying the lie, renouncing the lie, and replacing the lie with the truth. Ornella listened for the voice of the Lord. What was the lie she believed?

Her mind drifted back yet again to her five-year-old birthday party. Suddenly her father's booming voice and hateful words rose to her consciousness. "You're an imperfect, good-for-nothing. Not fit to be loved."

Imperfect. Unfit to be loved.

Ornella shuddered as a light exploded in her soul. She couldn't love Mara because in her eyes, Mara was imperfect. Not good enough to be loved. Just as her father had not loved her because in his eyes, she was imperfect. Not good enough to be loved.

Suddenly, the lie was as clear as day. Ornella believed

she had to be perfect in order to be loved. And she believed Mara had to be perfect in order to be loved.

A dam broke in Ornella's soul as tears gushed out of her eyes. "Oh, God, forgive me for believing the lie. I renounce it in the Name of Jesus, and I choose to embrace Your truth that I am loved without condition. Help me to love Mara without condition as well. In Your Name, Lord, I pray. Amen."

Like a geyser, hope erupted in Ornella's soul. The next day she would draw a sketch of Mara.

CHAPTER

SIXTEEN

ednesday, April 24, 1878

ORNELLA AWOKE the next morning with a new vision in her heart. For the first time since Mara's birth, hope danced in her soul. Something had happened inside her. The Lord had given her new eyes for her daughter. *His* eyes.

Mara greeted her with a lusty screech.

"Good morning, little one!" Ornella lifted her from the crib and settled into the rocking chair.

Mara gurgled and cooed, waving her little hands in the air.

193

Ornella took her waving hand. "What are you trying to tell me?"

Just then, Marco burst into the room. "There you are, Mama! I've been looking all over for you."

"And what exactly do you mean by 'all over'?"

"In the kitchen and the parlor."

"Well, doesn't 'all over' include my bedroom?"

Marco laughed, turning his full attention to Mara. "She's so cute, Mama." He gently took hold of his sister's hand. "I can't wait till she can play outside with us."

"That won't be for a few years, Marco. It takes time for babies to grow."

"Good morning, Mama!" Caterina hastened into the room, holding Sofia in her arms.

'Be careful, Caterina. Don't put the kitten too close to Mara. Kittens have a way of scratching without notice."

"I won't, Mama. But can I hold her closer so that Mara can see her?"

Ornella smiled. "Yes, you may."

Caterina held Sofia within Mara's sight. When Mara saw the kitten, she released a loud squeal. Ornella and the children burst into laughter.

Within minutes the other children had joined Ornella, accompanied by Francesco.

"I'll be leaving for the fields shortly, Ornella. I wanted to check on you before I leave."

She looked at her husband, her heart stirring with admiration and respect. "Thank you, Francesco."

He bent over to smile at Mara. "Good morning, little one! Papa has to go to work, but I'll see you tonight at dinner."

Mara screeched again, arousing great delight among all the family members.

Francesco took Ornella's hand. "What are your plans for today?"

She looked at him and smiled. "I'm going to do a sketch of Mara."

His eyebrows stretched upward toward his hairline. "That's wonderful!" The look on his face told Ornella that she'd removed a great load from his heart.

That afternoon, when the children were outside playing, Ornella decided to use the quiet time to draw a sketch of Mara. Ornella's body tensed. Could she bare to study closely the abnormal features of her Mongoloid child? Until this point, she'd averted them as much as possible. Sketching the baby's face meant studying every shape, every angle, every nuance, every shadow.

She swallowed hard. Anxiety gripped her soul, causing her to break out in a cold sweat. But she had promised God that she would choose to love Mara as He loved Mara. Unconditionally.

Gathering her sketch pad and some pencils, she took Mara upstairs to the bedroom and laid the child in the center of the large bed.

Mara's eyes widened at her new location in the big bed.

"You're probably wondering why I've put you here, aren't you?" Ornella smiled. "Well, I'm going to draw a picture of you, Mara. Would you like me to do that?"

The baby cooed and gurgled, kicking her little legs in delight.

Ornella laughed. "Let's have some fun, shall we?"

Mara emitted a loud gurgle that sounded like a laugh.

Encouraged by her baby's reaction, Ornella sat on the edge of the bed, laid her sketch pad on her lap, and, taking a pencil in hand, touched it to the blank page. Her fist tightened. Could she do this? Could she gaze at her daughter's abnormal face for more than a moment?

Whispering a prayer for courage, she drew the first line—the curved top of her baby's head. A surge of joy flooded Ornella's soul at the act of creating again. Oh, how she'd missed her art!

Holding her breath, she forced herself to look closely at Mara's face. The initial flash of repulsion quickly changed to wonder. Yes, there were abnormalities in the shape of her eyes and her nose, but there was also beauty in the contour of her cheeks and the shape of her chin. Why hadn't Ornella noticed those normal features before? She'd been so focused on what was wrong with Mara that she hadn't focused on what was right with her.

Slowly the tension in her hand subsided as Ornella yielded herself to the drawing process. All time ceased as the pencil in her hand danced over the page, carefully forming every line and shading flat shapes into three-dimensional ones. Mesmerized by the act of creating again, she was lost in another world where all time ceased. With her deft hand and her sharp eye, she captured every nuance of Mara's little face. Each pencil stroke was a loving caress that brought healing to her soul.

All the while, Mara lay quietly on the bed, watching Ornella intently. As Mara cooed and gurgled, Ornella hummed an old Italian tune. The baby joined in the singing with original sounds of joy and delight.

An hour later, Ornella's breath caught as she stared at the finished drawing. Had it truly emerged from her hand? So amazing was it that it sent chills coursing through her veins. The drawing resonated with something ethereal, other-worldly. Something sacred and divine. It may have come from her hand, but it had come from God's heart.

In that moment, Mama came looking for her. "What is Mara doing on the bed?"

Ornella smiled. "I just did a sketch of her." She handed it to Mama.

Upon seeing the sketch, Mama's eyes filled with tears. "This is absolutely stunning, Ornella. It has the hand of God drawn all over it."

A shiver went through Ornella. "You noticed that too, Mama?"

Mama handed the drawing back to Ornella.

"Ornella, God has anointed you to speak for Him through your art."

"Speak for God?" Who was wise enough to speak for God?

"Yes, *figlia mia*. God told the prophet Jeremiah that if he would extract the precious from the worthless, he would be God's spokesman. And so he was." Mama smiled, her eyes brimming with tears. "And so it is with you, Ornella. Through your art, you have extracted the precious truth of Mara's worth from the worthless lie that she does not deserve to be loved because of her imperfections."

Mama placed a hand on Ornella's shoulder. "God has many languages through which He speaks. The language may be writing, or drawing, or cooking, or farming. But in every case, He gives us the words to speak. Much as He does when we speak in tongues. Our duty is to yield to His words and to speak them through whatever gift He has given us."

Ornella nodded in understanding. "I was so afraid that He'd taken my gift of art away from me, Mama."

"*Figlia mia*, the Bible tells us that the gifts of God are irrevocable. Once He gives them, He never takes them back. It is Satan who tries to keep us from using our gifts for God's glory."

"But so many obstacles stood in the way, shouting at me to stop. To give up my art. First my unexpected pregnancy. Then Mara's abnormality."

Mama sat down on the bed next to Ornella, a gentle smile gracing her lips. "What looked like an obstacle was really a vehicle, Ornella. The vehicle to your destiny."

Ornella fingered the gold cross around her neck. "Just like the Cross, right? An obstacle to those who don't believe, but the vehicle to salvation to those who do."

Mama paused. "I have a feeling that Mara will become your artistic trademark and that you will bless many people through your paintings of her."

Mama's words sank deep into Ornella's heart and planted a new vision there. She and Mara would become an artistic team that would touch the world with the love and mercy of Christ. Through her paintings of Mara, Ornella would become God's spokeswoman, proclaiming His love, His mercy, and His compassion toward all those who suffer. When viewers gazed upon her paintings of Mara, they would be comforted as they experienced God's presence and help in their own times of trouble.

A sudden clap of thunder interrupted their conversation, startling Mara. She began to cry.

Laying her drawing aside, Ornella gathered her baby into her arms and held her close to her heart. All feelings of repulsion were gone. Only unconditional love remained.

The children burst into the bedroom. "Mama, it's raining. Can we have a snack?"

Ornella laughed. "Let me take care of Mara first, and then I'll get you something to eat."

Marco tugged on Ornella's sleeve. "Can we play with Mara, Mama?"

Ornella thought a moment. "I'll lay her blanket on the parlor floor and you can entertain her. But be careful you don't overwhelm her."

Caterina was quick to comment. "Yes, Marco. Did you hear that?"

Marco stuck out his tongue at Caterina. "Mara likes me better than you."

Ornella knit her brows together. "Now, Marco. That is not a nice thing to say to your sister. Remember, Mara is watching you and will imitate what you do. So be loving, do you hear me?"

Be loving. The words were for Ornella most of all. She had not been loving to the child of her womb. But from today onward, she would do everything in her power to prove to Mara that her mama loved her with no strings attached.

~

WEDNESDAY, April 24, 1878

SOON AFTER BIDDING farewell to Ornella and the children, Francesco arrived at the fields with relief flooding his heart. Ornella's decision to return to her art told him that she was on the mend. God had answered his prayer. The future looked bright, despite the challenges they would face raising Mara.

He checked on his growing tomato plants. They were progressing well and should yield a good harvest. Next he went to check on his men plowing the cornfields and preparing them for planting in late May.

A rustling sound behind him caught Francesco's attention. He turned to find William running hard toward him.

"Francesco, come quick! The barn is on fire!"

Francesco's heart lurched as he broke into a run toward the barn. "William, fetch the firefighters. I'm going to the barn."

William ran behind him. "Alex is on his way to town to fetch them."

Francesco's heart pounded as he approached the old burning building. Billows of gray-black smoke lifted into the air like thick puffs of smoke from a recently fired canon. "William, the mares! We've got to rescue the mares first."

The two horses were locked in their stalls where, during the cold season, they usually remained until feeding time. Also housed within the barn were the seeds for this year's planting, the fertilizer, hay to feed the horses, and the tools Francesco and William had recently repaired for use in the fields. If he lost it all, he would lose his livelihood. How would he take care of his family?

With William's help, Francesco struggled to open the large, double wooden barn doors. Its hinges creaked as the two men pried open both sides and pushed them back against the outer wall.

A sudden rush of heat and smoke slapped Francesco in the face, inciting an episode of intense coughing. His eyes watered and his nostrils stung. The sour taste of smoke coated his tongue, spreading nausea throughout his gut. Like shooting serpent's tongues, huge flames licked the aging wood and leaped toward the cloudless blue sky above. Sadly no chance of rain to quench their thirst.

"Be careful! And hurry!" Francesco shouted as he and William entered the burning structure and ran toward the stalls. "We've got only about two or three minutes to get them out. They may try to run back, so pull them out with all your strength."

Smoke filled the air. His lungs burned every time he took a breath. All around him, the crackling sound of burning wood and hay bombarded his ears as large chunks of wood broke from the roof and fell, landing only inches away.

To the right, the two mares stood in their stalls, their eyes wide with fear. Francesco threw open the stalls. He grabbed one old horse by the collar. "Come, girl!" He led her to safety while William led the other.

Francesco shouted above the noise of the raging flames. "Take the mares as far away as you can so they won't try to re-enter the barn. I'm going back in to retrieve as much of the seed and as many of the tools as I can."

"Francesco, wait!" William shouted. "You can't go in there alone!"

Francesco waved a hand at him. "Go! I'll be all right."

Just then, the fire wagon pulled up a short distance from the barn. Five firefighters jumped out and ran to the barn, only a few steps behind Francesco. "Let us handle it!"

Ignoring their warning, Francesco ran into the barn to rescue his seed. Without his seed for the spring and summer plantings, he had nothing. His life rested in those seeds.

Coughing incessantly as he breathed the putrid air, he stepped over several burning objects now strewn over the barn floor, trying hard not to burn his boots. As he neared the area where he stored his seed, his heart fell to his feet. Wild flames devoured the cartons of seeds—cucumbers, green beans, zucchini, and sweet corn—once neatly stacked in readiness for use. Not a single box remained intact.

Stunned, Francesco grabbed his thick hair with both hands and shouted. "My seed! All my seed is lost!"

A firefighter grabbed Francesco by the arm. "Get out of here now, before you lose your life as well."

Dazed and heartbroken, Francesco glanced over his shoulder as the firefighter pushed him from behind. "Hurry! The roof has begun to cave in!"

Francesco and the firefighter had barely reached the outside when the barn roof came crashing down. Its loud roar reverberated throughout the air as his whole life came crashing down around him as well.

CHAPTER
SEVENTEEN

ednesday, April 24, 1878

BY THE TIME the firefighters put out the fire, there was nothing left of the barn but an empty shell. Taking their leave, they expressed their sorrow at Francesco's loss and wished him well.

Upon seeing the smoke, Ornella, Mama, and the children had rushed to the field surrounding the barn. Neighbors had gathered to help douse the flames and now stood nearby, staring in awe at the charred remains of the old structure, offering whatever comfort they could.

When the excitement had ceased, the crowd dissipated and the farmhands returned to their plowing. After gathering their equipment, the firefighters left as well, while Mama took the children back to the house.

Her stomach lodged in her throat, Ornella stood alone beside Francesco, her hand in his, beholding with anguish the rubble and ashes of the building that once housed their livelihood. What would they do now? With no means of income and a new baby to care for, things looked bleak.

"I will have to find employment in town." A quiver lined Francesco's voice. "At least for the time being, until I can get the barn rebuilt and the supplies replaced."

"How long do you think that will take?"

"Several months. The neighbors have offered to help. Plowing season has already begun, but I now have no seed to plant. As for the rest of the summer planting, there will be none this year. We'll have to make do on what we have."

"But you have to pay your men."

"Yes. That comes first. They've been faithful and should not have to suffer because of this."

Ornella swallowed hard. "That leaves us with only two or three more months of provision."

His gaze riveted on her. "I know, Ornella. You don't need to remind me." Sharpness edged his voice.

She withdrew her hand from his. "I'm sorry,

Francesco. It's just that I'm worried. With another mouth to feed now . . ."

He cut her off. "Don't you think I'm aware of that? What kind of man do you think I am?"

"Francesco, I did not mean to offend you. I know you're upset, but please don't take it out on me." She paused, guilt overcoming her. He'd put up with her during her difficult time with Mara. Could she not now be patient with him in his distress? "I'm sorry, Francesco. Please forgive me." She paused. "I'm going home to make dinner." With that, she turned and headed for the path back to the house, leaving her husband alone with his pain.

The smell of smoke lingered in the afternoon sky, infecting every breath of air Ornella took. If only it would rain. A good rain would wash away the foul odor. But it could not wash away the sorrow in her heart.

The weight of the barn loss settled deep into her soul. How had the fire started? Francesco was very careful to keep everything in order. Daily he checked to ensure the safety of his horses and the items in the barn. He was known among the farmers in the area for taking extraordinary precautions to prevent fires. Many of those same farmers had come to help the firemen fight the blaze. Such was the unity among them.

As she walked back, her heart smarted over her recent ugly exchange with Francesco. Why hadn't she kept her mouth shut? She didn't need to remind him that they had an extra mouth to feed. Her comment had revealed a lack of trust in her husband. Remorse filled her.

Her gaze sought her house in the distance. Thank God it stood far enough away from the barn not to have been affected by the fire.

As she approached the house, she stopped. Another stray cat sat by the back door. Her heart stirred. But she couldn't take in any more strays, no matter how soft the spot in her heart for stray animals. Yet, this one was a beautiful calico kitten. Perfect for Caterina.

"All right, I'll bring you some milk. Just give me a minute."

Upon entering the kitchen, Ornella found Mama preparing dinner.

"Mama. What are you doing?"

"Cooking dinner." Concern flooded Mama's face. "Several neighbors have stopped by to inquire if we are all right. News about the fire is all over Cape May."

"I'm not surprised. People came all the way from town to see the fire for themselves."

Mama placed a hand on Ornella's arm. "How is Francesco?"

"Worried sick about what this loss will mean to us financially, especially now with Mara in the family."

Mama nodded. "God will provide, *figlia mia*. He always does."

Ornella retrieved a bowl from the cupboard and filled it with milk for the stray kitten. Upon hearing their mother's return, the children gathered around her in the kitchen.

"What are you doing, Mama?"

"Feeding another stray kitten."

Caterina squealed. "Oh, Mama. May I have her?"

"Actually, I was thinking she would make a good pet for you."

Marco cheered. "Now I won't have to share Sofia with you any longer."

As Caterina took over feeding the new stray kitten, the children hammered Ornella with questions.

"Is Papa going to build a new barn? How did the fire start? Will we have to move?" Question after question bombarded her, making her head spin.

"Children, one at a time, please."

The children quieted down.

"First of all, we are going to rebuild the barn. Several of the neighbors have offered to help. Second, I don't know how the fire started. And last, no, we will not have to move."

A sigh of relief came from Giovanni. "Thank God. I was so afraid we would have to leave the farm."

Ornella motioned her brood to come closer. "Always remember, children, the Bible tells us that God is a very present help in time of trouble. This means that He is always with us when trouble comes our way." She spoke far more to herself than to her children.

"He's always with us when trouble doesn't come our

way, too, Mama." Marco's smiling face warmed Ornella's heart.

"Yes, that is true, Marco. Now, let's thank God for protecting all of us, especially for protecting Papa. And let's ask Him to help us get through this trial."

And the many other trials that would come their way.

With her children gathered around her and Mama at her side, Ornella prayed a prayer of thanks for God's protection, requesting his help as they navigated the difficult days ahead.

~

WEDNESDAY, April 24, 1878

LATER THAT NIGHT, Francesco sat with Ornella in their bedroom, distraught with sorrow. How had the fire started? He'd been very careful to take every precaution to prevent such a catastrophe. The morning of the fire, he'd inspected the entire barn, and nothing seemed out of order.

"Francesco." Ornella's voice distracted him from his thoughts. "Do you know how the fire started?"

"It had to have been the hay."

"The hay? What do you mean?"

"When I ran into the barn, the hay bales were wet. I

hadn't noticed this on my inspection this morning. Hay in this condition can generate internal heat that can later ignite. I think that's what happened."

Worry lined Ornella's face. "How are we going to rebuild?"

"As you know, some of our neighboring farmers have offered to help me build a new barn." He turned toward her. "But I may have to dip into our savings again to purchase more seed. We will have to be very frugal for the next year."

As he spoke the words, he swallowed the hard lump of fear that had formed in his throat. Fear that he would resist with all his might. For the Bible told him that God had not given him a spirit of fear but of power, love, and a sound mind. He would trust in that promise.

"Perhaps I can take in some sewing."

Ornella's offer sounded sweet to his ears. But instead of agreeing to it, he offered her a suggestion in return. "Why don't you start painting again and sell your work?"

"But you yourself said that it might take a while before I sell anything?"

He lowered his head and then looked up again. "I know I did. But I've changed my mind. I think you should at least try, Ornella. Art is your passion. Your heart. And you must follow your heart."

For the first time in months, light flickered in Ornella's eyes.

The look of hope on her face warmed Francesco's

heart. It was worth whatever price he had to pay to get back on his feet and to restore his marriage. When Ornella was happy, he was happy.

And he would give his life to make her happy once again.

CHAPTER

EIGHTEEN

Two Months Later
Friday, June 21, 1878

To Ornella's relief, within weeks neighbors had helped rebuild the barn. Francesco had dipped into their savings yet again to purchase more seed so that he would have at least a small harvest.

Meanwhile, each day Ornella made it her goal to do one quick sketch of Mara. She sketched her baby sleeping, eating her first solid foods, and giggling with her siblings as she screeched at them at the top of her lungs. In the two months since she'd decided to sketch her daughter, Ornella had created a thick portfolio of sketches to use as the basis for oil paintings. This summer, Lord willing, she would begin to paint.

Each sketch revealed a new aspect of her child. Mara was a warm, happy child. The smallest things filled her with delight and wonder. She responded readily to her siblings' attention and seemed happiest when with them.

Having chosen to focus on what was right with Mara, Ornella had found delight in her child. Because of her late development in some areas, Mara could not hold her head erect, but she was able to sit, propped against the back of the sofa, without toppling over.

But today, seated with her children and Mama in the parlor, Ornella worried.

Mara was not her usual self. Her eyes no longer sparkled, and her demeanor had become subdued. She'd cried all morning and was listless in her interactions with her siblings. Worst of all, swelling had appeared in her little legs, in her belly, and around her eyes.

Ornella studied Mara as she lay sound asleep in her lap. Her lips had turned a pale shade of bluish-gray. Instead of the regular breathing that usually accompanied the baby's sleep, her breathing was rapid and labored.

Panic gripped Ornella's soul. "Giovanni. Please go to the fields and ask Papa to come home right away. Tell him there's a problem with Mara."

"Yes, Mama." In a moment, Giovanni was out the door.

Meanwhile, Caterina and Teresa gathered around their little sister. "Mama, why are Mara's lips blue?" So, her daughters had noticed, too.

"I don't know. As soon as Papa comes, we will take her to Dr. Gerken to find out."

In a few moments, Giovanni returned with Francesco close behind. Francesco rushed toward Ornella and the baby. Sweat trickled down his ruddy cheeks and onto his shirt. "What's the matter with Mara?"

"I'm not sure. But something is wrong. Her lips are blue and she's having trouble breathing."

Francesco took a look at his daughter. "We must go to Dr. Gerken right away. Giovanni, please go tell William to fetch the wagon."

"Yes, Papa."

In a few moments, Ornella, Francesco, and Mara were on their way to town. Francesco held the reins, while Ornella held Mara. The child was like a rag doll in her arms, her eyes closed and her breathing, labored.

Soon they reached Dr. Gerken's office. Situated on a little knoll toward the north end of town, the little office building stood like a sentinel of hope to the tiny community.

Holding Mara, still fast asleep in her arms, Ornella entered the office followed by Francesco. The room was empty except for an elderly gentleman seated in the far corner, reading a newspaper.

A receptionist greeted them with a smile. "Hello, Mr. and Mrs. Lombardi. How may I help you today?"

Francesco spoke. "Our daughter Mara is not well."

The receptionist took one look at Mara and nodded. "I'll notify Dr. Gerken immediately. Please be seated."

Ornella found two adjacent chairs and took one of them, while Francesco took the other. A chill ran through her blood as she imagined the worst. By now, Mara's breathing was even more labored.

"The doctor will see you now." The receptionist's voice was urgent.

Ornella sighed in relief. Holding the sleeping Mara close to her heart, Ornella entered the examining room, followed by her husband.

"Well, well, now. Whom do we have here?" The elderly doctor took Mara into his arms and studied her closely. As he held her, she awakened and stared at him.

He then placed her on the examining table and, all the while keeping his eyes on her, he asked questions of Ornella.

"When did you first notice the bluish lips? The labored breathing? The increasing listlessness?"

As best she could, Ornella answered the doctor's questions in detail.

Afterward, Dr. Gerken listened to little Mara's heart. After lifting the stethoscope from her chest, he turned toward Ornella and Francesco. "I'm sorry to tell you this, but I hear a serious heart defect."

Ornella's breath caught. "What do you mean, doctor?"

He paused to clear his throat before responding. "Mongoloid children frequently are born with heart problems that can be very serious."

Ornella looked at Mara, now awake and lying limply on the examining table. "How serious?"

The good doctor locked his gaze onto hers, a look of concern in his eyes. "They can be fatal."

Ornella's blood turned to ice. "Fatal?"

Dr. Gerken nodded. "Yes. Fatal."

Panic coiled its snaky grip around Ornella's heart and squeezed. "So, are you telling me that Mara is going to die?"

"Ornella, I am very sorry to have to say this, but Mara does not have long to live."

"But she's only six months old! She's barely begun to live!"

Dr. Gerken's face reflected deep compassion. "Many Mongoloid children die before their first birthday."

"But she can't die!" The words had no sooner escaped Ornella's lips than she realized the absurdity of them.

A tsunami of remorse washed over her. If only she'd been kinder to her child at the beginning. More sensitive to her needs. If only she'd not been so wrapped up in herself as to neglect—or worse yet—ignore her baby.

If only she'd loved her as Mara deserved to be loved.

A sob hitched in her throat. "But no one ever told me this."

Dr. Gerken looked at her with compassion. "There was no need to tell you. Some babies never develop symptoms. Moreover, I detected no problems until this point."

Francesco furrowed his brows. "Is there anything that can be done to alleviate her suffering?"

"Normally in cases of swelling, we apply leeches. But I would not recommend this treatment for an infant. Beyond that, there is nothing else."

Fear and guilt chased each other's tails in Ornella's soul. "You said she doesn't have long to live. What does that mean? One year? One month? One day?" While she needed to hear his response, she shut her heart to it.

Dr. Gerken sighed. "She could die at any time, but the longest I would predict is three months."

Three months. A meteor struck Ornella's soul. Her head spinning, she reached for Francesco's hand and gripped it.

"Doctor, what do we need to do at this point?" Although laden with sorrow, Francesco's voice was strong and stable.

"There is not much you can do medically. Just keep her well-nourished and as happy as you can. Most of all, love her."

Love her! That's what Ornella had done least of all.

Dr. Gerken nodded. "And of course, pray. Miracles still happen."

Ornella found it difficult to breathe under Dr. Gerken's medical verdict. Like a bursting dam, the bad news had unleashed torrents of fear in her heart. Spiraling downward into the dark abyss, she steadied herself as her head whirled in disbelief.

Dr. Gerken's eyes misted. "I'm sorry I don't have better news for you." He sighed. "Please schedule another appointment for next week. Meanwhile, if there is any change for the worse, bring her in right away." With that, he left the examining room.

Hot tears streaming down her face, Ornella picked up her little girl and squeezed her to her heart. Now that she was about to lose Mara, she realized how much she loved her and needed her. Her own pain had blocked that love, but God, in His power, had released it.

As Ornella followed Francesco out of the doctor's office, her only thought was saving Mara's life.

FRIDAY, June 21, 1878

ON THE WAY home from the doctor's office, Ornella held Mara close to her heart, while Francesco silently drove the wagon. Neither one of them spoke.

Was this just a bad dream, or was Mara really on the verge of death? Everything had happened so suddenly. One day Mara was fine. The next day she was on the verge of death.

Guilt washed over her at the awful memory of how she'd treated her baby. Had her failure to show Mara the love she'd needed brought on the child's illness? If so, Ornella would never forgive herself.

Her stomach twisted at the recollection of Dr. Gerken's somber prediction. At the most, Mara had only three months to live. Three short months. Surely he was mistaken.

Ornella tensed. Why was this happening? Had she committed some grave sin for which God was punishing her? After realizing the error of her ways, she'd repented and changed her behavior. Her relationship with Mara had greatly improved and was flourishing. Ornella had seen the truth and had begun to love Mara as her baby deserved to be loved—without condition. The future had looked bright again, and all was well with her world.

But it wasn't.

Ornella swallowed the bile that rose to her throat. *Why, God? Why now, after I'd repented and changed my ways. Why have things gotten worse instead of better? What cruel joke are You playing on me?*

Francesco interrupted her silent tirade. "Are you all right, Ornella?"

Choking back a sob, she turned toward him.

"Francesco, I'm so afraid. I can't bear the thought of losing Mara."

He shook his head. "I don't understand. Everything had turned for the better and things were going so well. And now this." His voice dropped.

Ornella rested her chin on Mara's little head. "What are we going to do?"

"We're going to pray for Mara's healing." Francesco's voice was resolute.

He pulled the wagon over to the side of the road. "Let's pray over her now as the Word commands us to do."

Holding Mara, Ornella gently leaned toward Francesco. Together, they laid hands on their precious baby and Francesco prayed.

"Father God, Your Word says that if we who believe in You and trust You lay hands on the sick, they shall recover. Not *might*, but *shall*. This is Your promise to us, Your children. So, in the Name of Jesus, we lay hands on our little Mara, Your gift to us. We speak Your Word over her that she was healed by the stripes of Jesus and that no weapon formed against her shall prosper. In the Name of Jesus, we command her heart to align with Your Word and to be made whole. In the Name of Jesus, we command every spirit of infirmity to leave her now. We thank You, Father, for Your faithfulness to Your Word. You cannot lie. You say what You mean, and You mean what You say. Therefore, in the Name of Jesus we pray, believe, and receive, confident that what You have promised, You will fulfill. Amen."

"Amen." As Ornella spoke the word of agreement, Mara opened her eyes and, for the first time that day, she smiled.

Faith surged through Ornella. She would not accept the doctor's verdict! No! A thousand times no! God was not the author of death but of life. His Word said so. She would fight for Ornella's life with every ounce of breath she had within her.

And she would not back down until Mara's body reflected the healing Jesus died to give her.

CHAPTER

NINETEEN

F*riday, June 21, 1878*

UPON ARRIVING HOME, Francesco went to the parlor where Mama and the children eagerly awaited their return, while Ornella went to change Mara's diaper and to feed her.

Francesco gathered his mother-in-law and the children around him to inform them of Mara's condition.

Wide-eyed with worry, the children listened as Francesco explained Dr. Gerken's diagnosis.

"Is Mara going to die, Papa?" Marco's eyes held fear.

"Mama and I prayed that the Lord would heal her, my son."

"When will she be healed, Papa?" Caterina's voice quivered.

"She is already healed, sweetheart."

Caterina quirked her brows. "But she still looks sick!"

"We must not focus on the symptoms but on God's Word. Jesus said that Mara was healed by His stripes. Jesus cannot lie. Mama and I have prayed for Mara, and we ask you to do the same. Jesus is the Healer, and He always heals when we ask Him in faith."

Marco drew his eyebrows together. "What's faith, Papa?"

"It's believing that when Jesus says something, He means it. When He makes a promise, He always keeps it."

Marco drew closer to Francesco. "Did Jesus promise to make Mara better, Papa?"

"Yes, Marco. He says in the Bible that we were healed when He took lashes on His back for our healing." Francesco paused. "But we must believe what Jesus said. It is our faith that enables us to receive His promises."

Marco exclaimed, "I believe, Papa."

Francesco smiled. "Bravo, Marco! God is pleased with you."

Giovanni raised his hand as though in school. "Papa, does Jesus heal everyone who believes that He will?"

"Yes, Giovanni. Jesus heals everyone who asks Him for healing in faith. Jesus has no favorites."

Marco turned to Caterina, a smug look on his face. "See, Caterina, it doesn't matter that you like Mara better than you like me. Jesus likes us both the same. So there."

Caterina scowled but remained silent.

Papa continued "Here is the secret, children. Jesus has already healed us. Healing is not in the future. It is now. If we are in Christ, we already have healing. But we must believe that Jesus has already healed us. Believing that He will heal us some time in the future is not faith. It is hope. Believing that Jesus has already healed us is faith. If we don't have faith, God is not pleased with us."

A somber look crossed the children's faces.

Teresa spoke. "But, Papa, you and Mama prayed. Yet, Mara doesn't look any better. She looks worse."

"You make an excellent point, Teresa. Listen to what the Scriptures say in Mark 11: 24: "Therefore I say unto you, What things soever ye desire, when ye pray, believe that ye receive them, and ye shall have them." This verse tells us that we must believe that we receive our healing at the moment we pray. Then, some time after we pray, we shall see that healing demonstrated in our bodies."

Giovanni scratched his head. "It's confusing, Papa. How can you say Mara is healed when she doesn't look healed?"

"She will eventually look healed, Francesco. Between the time we pray in faith and the time the healing manifests in her body, Satan will try to get us to doubt God's Word. Satan often makes things look worse before they look better. But if we hold on to what God promised, we shall see His promise come to pass in our lives."

Giovanni scrunched his nose. "It seems like a lot of work to me, Papa."

Papa chuckled. "It's a fight, Giovanni. The Bible calls it the good fight of faith."

Marco quirked an eyebrow. "Why is it a *good* fight, Papa? Seems pretty bad to me."

Papa smiled. "It's a good fight, Marco, because we have already won the battle through Jesus."

Just then Ornella entered the room, carrying Mara.

A hush fell over the children as Ornella took a seat beside Francesco and smiled. "Mara wants to see her siblings."

Caterina ventured closer. "Hi, Mara." She took her sister's little hand and squealed with delight as Mara wrapped her little fingers around Caterina's thumb. Caterina grinned at Ornella.

One by one, the children drew closer. In turn, each offered a comforting word. "We're praying for you, Mara," Teresa assured her.

"We love you, Mara," Marco exclaimed.

"Next winter, I'll take you out sledding," Giovanni added with a flourish.

Francesco took Ornella's hand and squeezed it.

Everything was going to be all right, no matter what the circumstances looked like. God was with them and would never leave them nor forsake them. That was His promise.

And Francesco believed it!

~

MONDAY, June 24, 1878

AS THE DAYS PASSED, Mara's condition worsened. Because of her increasing labored breathing, she could barely sleep at night. Her little body swelled even more, and her listlessness increased. The situation did not look good. It was time to fetch Dr. Gerken.

The sharp claws of fear dug into Ornella's heart and soul as Mara lay limp in her arms. Her baby was close to death. Only a miracle would save her.

Suddenly nothing seemed important anymore except Mara's survival. Ornella would give up anything—even her dream of art—to have Mara live. Bursting into tears, she fell to her knees and cried out to God. "O God of Heaven and Earth, I plead with You on behalf of my baby. I don't deserve Your grace, but I implore You to grant it. Turn the tide and let my baby live. I surrender Mara to You, Lord. She was Yours before she was mine. She belongs to You, Lord." Ornella lowered her head. "I surrender my will to Yours, O Lord." A deep peace settled over her.

Still, one after another, the enemy's fiery darts struck Ornella's mind, taunting her with lies about God and His Word. It took every ounce of strength left within her to deflect those arrows with the Sword of the Spirit, God's Holy Word. The battle was intense, but the victory assured. As long as she held on in faith.

Terrified that Mara would soon breathe her last, Ornella placed the infant on her bed and knelt beside her. Tears streamed down Ornella's face as she continued her plea before the God of the Universe. Fingering the gold cross her grandmother had given her, Ornella whispered her Nonna's words to her those many years ago: *In times of trouble, always remember the Cross.* The Cross was not only a symbol of forgiveness but a symbol of physical healing as well.

Her heart crying out to God, Ornella lay her forehead on the bedspread, next to Mara's little body. Suddenly, Ornella heard a loud gurgle as a tiny hand touched the top of her head.

Her heart pounding, Ornella looked up at Mara's face, now glowing with life. Pink cheeks. Rosy lips. Clear, sparkling eyes. A face that held a beautiful, unearthly smile. A face that was no longer repulsive to Ornella despite the abnormal features. A face Ornella wanted to cradle and caress in her maternal hands, kissing every inch of it.

Lifting her now healthy baby from the bed, Ornella hurried downstairs to the parlor where Francesco, Mama, and the children were gathered.

"Praise the Lord!" she shouted. "God has given us a miracle! Mara is healed!"

The children exploded into shouts of praise while Francesco and Mama rushed to Ornella's side.

As Ornella gazed upon her little baby's face, she whispered, "Thank You, Jesus! Thank You for Your faithfulness to Your Word."

CHAPTER

TWENTY

T *uesday, June 25, 1878*

THE NEXT MORNING, Ornella, Francesco, and the children set out to pay a visit to Dr. Gerken. Holding Mara securely on her lap, Ornella sat in the wagon seat to the right of Francesco while the children settled in the back of the wagon.

Caterina's voice echoed from behind. "Marco, it's my turn to sit on the side. You have to sit in the middle."

"You sat on the side last time."

"I did not."

Ornella turned her head toward the back of the wagon. "Children, this is no time to argue. Settle this between yourselves immediately, or you will not be permitted to go to the carnival."

A hush quickly ensued as Caterina and Marco amicably worked out the seating arrangements between themselves.

As Francesco took the reins, Ornella smiled. It was amazing what children would do when they had a strong enough motive.

A light rain drizzled from a cloudy, gray sky, sprinkling the earth with its rhythmic pitter-patter. The sound was like music to Ornella's ears. She took a deep breath of the cool air, redolent with the sweet and musky fragrance of freshly-cut hay.

Soon the wagon pulled out of the driveway and onto the main road toward town. Ornella's heart stirred with excitement in anticipation of Dr. Gerken's reaction when he learned of Mara's miraculous healing. Would he be as overjoyed as she? Would he doubt or question the healing? Would he be measured in his reaction, not willing to commit either way?

After thirty minutes, they reached Dr. Gerken's office. Francesco parked the wagon in front, and one by one, the children climbed out of the back. Francesco helped Ornella and Mara from the front seat, and they all entered the little office building.

Upon seeing the entire family, the receptionist looked concerned. "Are you here on an urgent call regarding Mara?"

Ornella smiled. "Yes, but not urgent in the way you may think."

The receptionist knit her brows.

Ornella unwrapped the little blanket around Mara.

The receptionist took one look at her and lifted her gaze, her eyes round as saucers. "She looks wonderful!"

"Jesus healed her!" The joyful words spilled from Ornella's soul.

The receptionist's jaw dropped. "Follow me. Dr. Gerken is in his private office reviewing charts."

Ornella followed the receptionist to Dr. Gerken's private office while Francesco and the children trailed behind her.

The office door was wide open.

"Excuse me, Dr. Gerken." The receptionist gently interrupted him. "Mr. and Mrs. Lombardi are here to talk with you."

Dr. Gerken looked up. Upon seeing Ornella, he rose, a concerned look on his face. He came from behind his desk and greeted Ornella, Francesco, and the children.

"Mara has worsened." His words were a resigned statement.

Ornella could barely contain her joy. "No. Not at all." She took a deep breath. "Dr. Gerken, we've received a miracle."

"A miracle?" He gave her a questioning look.

Francesco explained. "Yes. Jesus healed our little

Mara. She no longer has any symptoms of heart problems."

A skeptical look on his face, Dr. Gerken lifted Mara from Ornella's arms and took her into his. "Let's go to my examining room. I want to take a closer look."

Tenderly, he carried Mara into his examining room. She cooed and gurgled in his arms, swatting him with her little hands.

He laid her on the examining table and studied her closely. He listened to her heart and her lungs. He checked her eyes, her lips, her belly, and her legs, shaking his head in disbelief the entire time. No more swelling in her limbs. No more bluish tint to her lips. No more labored breathing.

Finally, he raised his gaze toward Ornella, his eyes brimming with tears. "Your Mara is a healthy baby. There is nothing wrong any longer with her heart. Glory to God. You have, indeed, experienced a miracle. May your little one live long and strong on this earth."

On impulse, Ornella gave Dr. Gerken a big hug. "Thank you, Doctor Gerken. Thank you! We give God all the glory for His goodness."

"Amen!" Dr. Gerken then gave Francesco a hearty shake of the hand and tousled the heads of Giovanni and Marco. "Now you all take good care of that little sister of yours, do you hear?"

"Yes, Doctor Gerken!" Beaming with joy, the children replied in unison.

With that, Ornella, Francesco, and the children left the office and made their way back home.

As they neared the farm, Ornella looked up at the sky. A brilliant rainbow spanned the horizon, curving its glorious arc from east to west. The sign of God's everlasting covenant. The emblem of His Presence.

Tears streamed down her cheeks. In her heart of hearts, she thanked the God of Abraham, Isaac, and Jacob for His faithfulness. Never again would she fear trusting Him. Never again would she doubt His goodness. Never again would she question His love.

EPILOGUE

T*hree Years Later*
Saturday, May 14, 1881

WITH GREAT JOY spilling out of her heart, Ornella mingled among the many visitors who had come from far and wide to celebrate the grand opening of the Mara Art Gallery in downtown Cape May. By God's grace, the storefront she'd originally wanted to rent had become available again, and her art sales over the past two years had enabled her to rent it.

Several newspapers—local, regional, and national— had been advertising the big event for the past several weeks, with the result that the news had spread among artists and art lovers throughout the entire East Coast and beyond. To Ornella's great delight, the turnout was far beyond what she had expected.

During the past week, Francesco, Teresa, Caterina, Giovanni, and Marco had helped her clean the gallery and prepare it for the opening. Even Mama had played an important part by preparing some of her best Italian pastries for the guests. Now Ornella's entire family roamed around the large room, with big smiles on their faces, greeting visitors and serving refreshments.

Little Mara toddled at Ornella's side, her face beaming with delight. The star of the show, Ornella's little girl had endeared herself to thousands of art lovers all over the world through the many paintings of her that Ornella had created and sold. Paintings that had been recognized by experts in the art world as daring and brilliant in terms of subject matter, emotion, and technique. In a time when Mongoloid children were often ostracized and isolated in institutions, Ornella had presented another side to the issue. A more human side in which the Mongoloid child was honored as a human being worthy of the same respect as anyone else.

While many of Ornella's paintings had been sold and now hung in museums, offices, and homes around the world, some of them now hung on her gallery walls and rested on the easels artfully arranged throughout the bright and spacious room.

An elderly gentleman with a white beard approached Mara. Bending down to her level, he offered her his hand.

"I am so honored finally to meet you in person, Miss Mara."

Mara gave him a warm smile and grabbed hold of his beard. "Fuzzy. Mara likes it." She laughed with glee.

The man laughed and then straightened to address Ornella. "Your paintings of your precious child have brought healing to my soul." Tears glistened in his eyes. "My late wife and I lost a son to Mongoloidism soon after his birth. While he was alive, we experienced much opposition and criticism because we chose to care for him ourselves instead of placing him in an institution. Your paintings have brought a peace to my soul that I never knew I could regain. Thank you."

A lump formed in Ornella's throat. "Thank you, sir. I praise God for using my art to bless you."

"Indeed, He has."

One after another, visitors came up to Ornella to comment on her work and to thank Mara for being such an amazing subject of Ornella's paintings. Accompanied by Marco and Giovanni, Mara walked around the room, clapping her hands in delight and smiling at all who greeted her.

Ornella's heart filled with gratitude. Her little Mara—the child whom she'd once considered an obstacle—had instead become the vehicle to the fulfillment of her dream. And not only to her dream, but to the dream of many others who'd lost hope because of the obstacles in their own lives.

Ornella swallowed hard. As the prophet Isaiah decreed, God's thoughts were truly higher than her thoughts. His ways truly higher than her ways.

As Ornella moved slowly around the room, engaging each of her visitors one by one, her heart warmed at the goodness and faithfulness of God. He'd promised to give her the desires of her heart. Now she finally understood that what God meant was that He would put His desires in her heart, and she would want what He wanted for her. And so would her will become one with His. In this oneness did true surrender consist.

As the afternoon activities wound down, Francesco came up to Ornella and whispered in her ear. "I am so happy for you, my love. This is indeed a wonderful dream come true."

Ornella's heart warmed. She smiled and took her husband's hand. "I often doubted I would see this day, but God is faithful to His Word."

Little Mara ran up to her papa. "Papa! Papa!"

Francesco scooped her up into his arms and gently poked a finger into her belly. "And you, precious one, were the catalyst for it all."

Just as Mama had predicted.

Mara released a loud screech followed by the most beautiful smile Ornella had ever seen. She then clapped her hands and shouted, "Me Mawa! Me Mawa!"

The visitors stopped, turned toward her, and smiled, many with tears in their eyes.

As Ornella blinked back the tears in her own eyes, she silently thanked her Father in Heaven for showing her that all things work together for good to those who love the Lord.

THE END

AUTHOR'S NOTE: If you enjoyed this story, please consider leaving a review on Amazon, Goodreads, and BookBub. Reviews help other readers decide which books to purchase. Thank you!

If you are interested in learning of my future book releases, in receiving discounts on my books, and in being eligible for freebies and giveaways, please subscribe to my monthly author newsletter at the link below:

https://landing.mailerlite.com/webforms/landing/x5i2r2

Also, please follow me on the social media sites below:

Goodreads

https://www.goodreads.com/author/show/6592603.MaryAnn_Diorio

BookBub

https://www.bookbub.com/profile/maryann-diorio

Facebook

https://www.facebook.com/maryanndioriofiction/

Instagram

https://www.instagram.com/drmaryanndiorio/

X (formerly Twitter)

https://twitter.com/DrMaryAnnDiorio

A NOTE FROM THE AUTHOR

Thank you, dear reader, for taking precious time out of your life to read my story. I trust that it blessed you.

There are two points I wish to make clear regarding this story:

First, lest you be offended by my use of the term "Mongoloid," please be aware that this was the term used for Down syndrome in the late 19th century during which the story takes place. The term "Down syndrome" did not come into usage until the early 1970s. So, in order to remain true to the historical time period, I used the term "Mongoloid."

Second, *The Farmer and Mrs. Lombardi* includes a miracle healing. Sad to say, I was severely criticized for including this healing in my story. The reason given by a well-meaning, early reader was that doing so would upset readers who'd prayed for healing and weren't healed.

But I could not in conscience deny the Word of God nor my own personal experience. Please allow me to share both with you.

FIRST, the Word of God . . .

God makes clear in His Word that healing is in the Atonement. God not only is able to heal us; He *wants* to heal us. And even more than that, He has already healed us.

When Jesus took the 39 lashes on His back just before being crucified, He paid for our healing. He took our sickness and disease and, in exchange, gave us His health.

Let's look at some Scripture verses that reveal this truth:

___*Matthew 8: 17 - "That it might be fulfilled which was spoken by Esaias the prophet, saying, Himself took our infirmities, and bare our sicknesses."*

Notice Jesus "took our infirmities" and "bare our sicknesses" so that we would not have to bear them.

___*Psalm 103: 2-3 - "Bless the LORD, O my soul, and forget not all his benefits: Who forgiveth all thine iniquities; who healeth all thy diseases . . . ."*

Notice: God heals ALL our diseases; not some, but ALL.

—-*Mark 11: 24 - "Therefore I say unto you, What things soever ye desire, when ye pray, believe that ye receive them, and ye shall have them."*

Notice: If we believe *when* we pray, then we receive what we prayed for the instant we pray for it. But the manifestation of our prayer often comes later. For example, I believe that I receive healing the instant I pray for it, but the healing may not show up in my body until a little while later.

God's will for healing is clear in the verses cited above, and in many other verses throughout the Sacred Scriptures.

SECOND, a Word on Faith . . .

How do we receive healing? By faith. Let's look at Scripture verses that reveal this:

__*Mark 5: 34 - "And he said unto her, 'Daughter, thy faith hath made thee whole; go in peace, and be whole of thy plague.'"*

In the story of the woman with the issue of blood, Jesus said that it was her faith that made her whole.

Jesus said the same of the blind man named Bartimaeus. His faith healed him.

__*Mark 10: 52 - "And Jesus said unto him, Go thy way; thy faith hath made thee whole. And immediately he received his sight, and followed Jesus in the way."*

So it is with us. Our faith makes us whole.

Jesus says what He means and He means what He says. Why, then, do we not take Him at His Word?

Third, My Personal Experience . . .

When my younger daughter was two months old, she was diagnosed with an incurable disease. The medical prognosis was that she would not live beyond nine years of age.

Because my husband and I knew and believed the Word of God on healing, we refused to accept our daughter's diagnosis. Instead, we laid hands on her as the Word commands, and we prayed for her healing.

Shortly after my husband and I prayed, our daughter's symptoms began to disappear. We took her back to her pediatrician, who was amazed and vouched for her healing.

Today our daughter is 47 years old, happily married, and serves on the worship team at her church. God's Word works!

Why do I share this? Because I am saddened to see so many people needlessly enduring sickness that Jesus took from them, simply because they do not know the truth about healing.

I am saddened by the false teaching about healing and the lack of teaching about healing in the Church. I am saddened from grieving over the untimely death of family members and friends who did not know the Word of God on healing or, worse yet, doubted it. Yes, all of us must die one day, but we don't have to be sick in order to die.

We have no problem believing that we are forgiven when we ask God to forgive us. Why? Because we have heard the message of forgiveness over and over and over again.

But we have trouble believing that we are healed. Why? Because we have *not* heard the message of healing over and over and over again. In fact, we've barely heard it at all!

Romans 10: 17 tells us that faith comes in only one way: by hearing, and hearing the Word of God. If we don't hear the Word of God on healing, we will never have faith for it.

Lest I mention only my daughter's healing for which we continue to praise God, I would like to share two more healings in my immediate family:

1) I was healed of breast cancer 30 years ago.

2) My husband was recently healed of cancer.

Why were we healed? Because we simply believed God's Word about healing.

It grieves me that so many churches today are reluctant to preach healing for fear of making people feel bad if they are not healed. I call this reluctance the *fear of man*. And God warns us against the fear of man.

I, for one, will not deny God's Word because of the fear of man. Instead, I will speak the truth in love because of my fear of God and my love for my fellow man. If we love someone, we will tell him the truth, regardless of how it makes him feel, because only the truth sets us free. If I do not receive something that God has promised me, the problem is with me, not with God.

So, my friend, if you are facing an illness today, the truth is that Jesus died to heal you as well as to forgive you. Choose to believe God's Word about healing.

Just as we cannot earn forgiveness of sin, neither can we earn physical healing. We simply believe that forgiveness and healing are ours, and we receive them with thanksgiving.

Our Lord Jesus Christ paid the ultimate price so that we can be free in spirit, soul, and body. We must not take His sacrifice lightly by not believing Him and by not receiving what He did for us. To do so would break His heart.

RECIPE FOR STRUFOLI

STRUFOLI
(Christmas Honey Balls)

INGREDIENTS:

1 tablespoon sugar
1 teaspoon grated lemon peel
1 teaspoon vanilla
1/2 teaspoon salt
4 eggs
2 1 /2 cups flour
Oil for frying
1 cup honey

Candy sprinkles or jimmies

INSTRUCTIONS:

__In a mixing bowl, combine sugar, lemon peel, vanilla, and salt.

__Add eggs and 2 cups flour; mix well.

__Turn onto a floured surface and knead in remaining flour (dough will be soft).

__With a floured knife, cut into 20 pieces. __With hands, roll each piece into a cylinder about 1/2 to 3/4 inch diameter.

__Cut each cylinder into 1/2 inch pieces.

__In a large skillet, heat oil to 350º.

__Fry pieces, a few at a time, for 2 minutes per side or until golden brown.

__Drain on paper towels.

__Place in a large bowl.

__Heat honey to boiling; pour over balls and mix well.

__With a slotted spoon, spoon onto a serving platter and slowly mound into a tree shape, if desired.

__Decorate with candy sprinkles.

__Allow to cool.

Yield: about 15 dozen. ENJOY!

About the Author

MaryAnn Diorio writes award-winning fiction from a quaint, small town in New Jersey where neighbors still stop to chat while walking their dogs, families and friends still gather on wide, wrap-around porches, and the charming downtown still finds kids licking lollipops and old married folks holding hands. A Jersey girl at heart, MaryAnn loves Jersey diners, Jersey tomatoes, and the Jersey shore.

You can learn more about MaryAnn and her writing at maryanndiorio.com.

ACKNOWLEDGMENTS

No book is written in isolation. All books represent the joint efforts of many people. This novel is no different.

I would like to express my deep gratitude to the following people who provided valuable research information and moral support during the writing of this story.

First, my heartfelt gratitude goes to my Lord and Savior Jesus Christ and His Holy Spirit. Thank You for trusting me with the story of Your heart.

Next, my deep love and respect go to my awesome husband Dom who prayed me through this book, who did the grocery shopping, the cleaning, and the cooking while I spent time in the "zone." And, as if that were not enough, he also did a thorough edit of my manuscript, reading through it several times. His attention to detail, his understanding of cause-and-effect, and his meticulous historical research contributed greatly to the technical aspects of this story.

My precious daughters, Dr. Lia Diorio Gerken and Gina Diorio Pope, encouraged me along the way through their love, their humor, and their prayers. Without question, I have the best daughters in the universe.

My deepest gratitude also goes to my powerful prayer partners who prayed with me through each obstacle that came against the writing and publishing of this story. And they were many! I would especially like to thank Sandra Marrongelli, Dr. Adeola Darden, Devata White, Barbara Hart, Christine Strittmatter, and Joan Gangwer. Your faithful, fervent prayers availed much and helped to birth this story. Thank you!

Thank you to my amazing Beta readers who took precious time out of their busy lives to read and offer valued comments. Your input made this a better book.

Thanks to my outstanding Book Launch Team for helping to spread the word about this book.

Thank you to the best Reader Team a writer could ever ask for. Your support of my writing keeps me going.

A special thanks to Jaye and Kathleen Paul and to Pamela and the late John Schiano for their invaluable help as parents of a precious Down syndrome child. Your willingness to share your hearts helped to make this a more authentic book. Blessings to you!

Thank you to the Facebook Group, CAPE MAY GOOD TIMES, and in particular to Richard Gibbs and Edward Runyan, director of Cape May County Park Zoo, for their expert help on farming in Cape May during the late 1800s.

Thank you to book designer, Hannah Linder, for designing the cover of this book.

Thank you to my professional editor for your expert help. I honor your wish to remain anonymous.

ALSO BY MARYANN DIORIO

Other Fiction by MaryAnn Diorio

The Madonna of Pisano

A Sicilian Farewell

Return to Bella Terra

In Black and White

Miracle in Milan

The Captain and Mrs. Vye

The Rabbi and Mrs. Goldstein

Surrender to Love

A Christmas Homecoming

A Daddy for Christmas

Fire-Engine Love

The Antique Clock

The Trunk in the Attic

Dixie Randolph and the Secret of Seabury Beach

Penelope Pumpernickel: Precocious Problem-Solver

Penelope Pumpernickel: Dynamic Detective

Penelope Pumpernickel: Mystery Maven

Who Is Jesus?

Candle Love

Toby Too Small

Do Angels Ride Ponies?

Poems for Wee Ones

The Dandelion Patch

Miracle at Madville

MaryAnn's books are available at https://maryanndiorio.com/
book-store-2/

HOW TO LIVE FOREVER

Eternal life is a free gift offered by God to anyone who chooses to accept it. All it takes is a sincere sorrow for your sins (contrition) and a quality decision to turn away from your sins (repentance) and begin living for God.

In John 3:3, Jesus said, "Unless a man is born again, he cannot see the Kingdom of God." What does it mean to be "born again"? Simply put, it means to be restored to fellowship with God.

Man is made up of three parts: spirit, soul, and body (I Thessalonians 5:23). Your spirit is who you really are; your soul is comprised of your mind, your will, and your emotions; and your body is the housing for your spirit and your soul. You could call your body your "earth suit."

When we are born into this world, we are born with a spirit that is separated from God. As a result, it is a spirit without life because God alone is the source of life. You may have heard this condition referred to as "original sin." Why is every human being born with a spirit separated from God? Because of the sin of our first parents, Adam and Eve.

I used to wonder why I had to suffer because of the sin of Adam and Eve. After all, I complained, I wasn't even there when they ate the apple! Yet as I began to understand spiritual matters, I began to see that I was there just as a man and woman's children, grandchildren, great-grandchildren, and so on, are in the body of the man and woman in seed form before those descendants are actually born. In other words, in my children there is already the seed for their future children. In their future children will be the seed of their future children, and so on.

Now, as a parent, I can pass on to my children only what I am and what I possess. For example, if I speak only Chinese, I can pass on to my children only the Chinese language. I possess no other language to give them out of my own self. The same was true with Adam and Eve. Because they disobeyed God, their fellowship with God was broken. Therefore, their spirits died because they were severed from God. As a result, they could pass on to their children only a dead spirit—a sinful spirit separated from God. And Adam and Eve's children could pass on to their children only a dead, sinful spirit. And so on, all the way down to you and me.

We said earlier that your spirit is the real you—who you really are. So what does it mean when your spirit—the real you—is separated from God? It means that unless you are somehow reconciled to God, you will go to hell after you die. Hell is a real place of real torment resulting from separation from God.

Now God is a holy God and He will not tolerate sin in His presence. At the same time, He is a loving God. Indeed, He IS Love! And because He loves you so much, He wanted to restore the broken relationship between you and Himself. He wanted to restore you to that glorious position of walking and talking with Him and enjoying the fullness of His blessings.

But there was a problem. Because God is infinite, only an infinite being could satisfy the price of man's offense against God. At the same time, because man committed the offense, there had to be someone who would also be able to represent man in paying this price. In other words, there had to be a being who was both God and man in order that the price for sin could be paid.

Since God knew that there was nothing man could do on his own to pay the price for his sin, God took the initiative. In the writings of John the Apostle, we learn that "God so loved the world that He gave His only-begotten Son, that whoever believes in Him shall not perish but have eternal life" (John 3:16).

What glorious GOOD NEWS! God loved you so

much that He sent His own and only Son, Jesus Christ, to take the rap for your sins. Imagine that! Would you give your son to go to the electric chair for someone else? Well, that's exactly what God did! The Cross was the electric chair of Christ's day, and God gave His own Son, Jesus Christ, to go to the Cross for you!

In dying on the Cross for you, and in rising from the dead three days later, Jesus paid the price for your sins and repaired the breach between you and God the Father. Jesus restored the broken relationship between man and God. He provided mankind with the gift of eternal life.

So what does all of this mean for you? It means that if you accept Christ's gift of eternal life, you will be "born again." In other words, God will replace your dead spirit with a spirit filled with His life. "Therefore, if anyone is in Christ, he is a new creation. Old things have passed away; behold, all things have become new" (2 Corinthians 5:17).

If I offer you a gift, it is not yours until you choose to take it. The same is true with the gift of eternal life. Until you choose to take it, it is not yours. In order for you to be born again, you must reach out and take the gift of eternal life that Jesus is offering you now. Here is how to receive it:

"Lord Jesus, I come to You now just as I am— broken, bruised, and empty inside. I've made a mess of my life, and I need You to fix it. Please forgive me of all of my sins. I accept You now as my personal Savior and as the Lord of my life. Thank You for dying for me so that I might live. As I give you my life, I trust that You will make of me all that You've created me to be. Amen."

If you prayed this prayer, please write to me to let me know. I will send you some information to help you get started in your Christian walk. Also, I encourage you to do three important things:

1) Get a Bible and begin reading in the Gospel of John.

2) Find a good church that preaches the full Gospel. Ask God to lead you to a church where you will be fed.

3) Set aside a time every day for prayer. Prayer is simply talking to God as you would to your best friend.

I congratulate you on making the life-changing decision to accept Jesus Christ! It is the most important decision of your life. Mark down this date because it is the date of your spiritual birthday. Be assured of my prayers for you as you grow in your Christian walk. God bless you!